octopus pie
volume 3

by Meredith Gran

Published by Image Comics, Inc. Office of publication:
2001 Center Street, Sixth Floor, Berkeley, CA 94704.

Printed in the USA. For information regarding the CPSIA on this printed material call: 203-595-3636 and provide reference #RICH–674908.

For international rights, contact: foreignlicensing@imagecomics.com.

ISBN: 978-1-63215-723-2

www.octopuspie.com

Interior designed by Meredith Gran and Kou Chen.
Cover art colors by Valeria Halla.

For Mike, to whom I wish to dedicate way more than books. But also this book.

Thanks to Kou Chen for an enormous amount of help laying out these pages, and to the School of Visual Arts for the chance to advise a new wave of talent.

WHERE'S MY **BOY?**

OH, **THERE'S** MY BOY.
COME LOVE ME.

DOES MANUEL **EVEN LOVE** ME?
DOES HE **HATE** ME?

...HE
HATES
ME!

NO.
I'LL
DIE.

ACK!
GURGLE
SPUTTER

DEAD
FOREVER

DID YOU
WANT TO GET
OUT OF THE
HOUSE, EVE?

I fell in love when I moved back to New York, and it was different. Really different. The kind of love that defines all future loves, and kills, rends, invalidates the ones of the past.

Finding that missing piece, that little key to the universe, meant salting the earth. Looking back became unbearable; I wondered what the road I'd been traveling was even **doing** there. I wanted to forget my transitional self, the one who blindly mistook the pleasant for the sublime. How was that version of me even **real**? How could a real person not know how to love? Now that I knew (and now that I was **real**), life could finally begin.

Death is a major theme in this book: death of the body, the home, friendships, routines, memories, career goals, institutions. And there's a lightness to it, a reassurance that death is the best remedy. Our heroes can break their lease over a vague feeling of anxiety. Eve can be cartoonishly murdered on Halloween as a form of reinvention. Marigold's heart can shatter and reform over tea a thousand times. It's fine. New beauty will grow from it.

I found beauty during the creation of this book. I made new friends and opened up to existing ones. I went on trips I'll never forget. I was inspired to exercise and test the limits of my body, and I felt a great sense of truth and belonging. What I wanted out of life had never seemed so close. And these characters, in turn, pursued their desires in more reckless ways. Not even death could hurt them.

The relationship ended, coincidentally, just before the end of this book. My friends of that period moved away. There was a brand new emptiness, one that no amount of experience or self-awareness can force you to confront. I felt the madness of lonesome, individual loss. It was an unfixable problem. Falling in love - for real, this time - had been easy. Watching it die was a descent into the underworld.

The road was intact, though. It stretched before a version of myself I thought I'd erased. It was a person I didn't love yet, but this time I knew how. This was, for the thousandth time, the beginning.

-Meredith Gran
March 2016

Contents

25
bags

IT'S HALLOWEEN IT'S HALLOWEEN IT'S TIME FOR SCARES IT'S TIME FOR SCREAMS
IT'S HALLOWEEN IT'S HALLOWEEN!

THE GHOSTS WILL SPOOK THE SPOOKS WILL SCARE--

HAS THERE ALWAYS BEEN A DOOR
NEXT TO THIS DOOR?

LOOK AT ALL THIS... THIS...
THAT'S RIGHT, EVE. SPACE.
1400 SQUARE FEET OF IT.
PLUG-INS GALORE. AND A CITY-FACING WINDOW.
HOW IS IT EVEN POSSIBLE, SAM ROCK-WELL?
NOT ONLY IS IT POSSIBLE.
IT'S BEEN RIGHT UNDER YOUR NOSE.
I HAD *THE DREAM* LAST NIGHT.

THE DOOR WAS RIGHT THERE. AND INSIDE WAS THIS HUGE ROOM WITH--
OH MY GOD.
SHE HAD THE BJORK DREAM TOO, HANNA!
YOU MEAN THE STARDUST-ERA BOWIE DREAM-- BUT YES.
IT IS AS I FEARED.
WE ALL HAD THE SAME DREAM?
IT'S A TRINITY OF BACK-DOOR COMPULSION. A WARNING FROM OUR COLLECTIVE UNCONSCIOUS.
THIS PLACE IS NO LONGER OUR HOME. WE MUST LEAVE.
G-G-G-G-G-GHOSTS?
BUT THERE'S A MONTH LEFT ON THE LEASE. AND I FIGURED WE'D STAY FOR--
THERE'S NO TIME, NING!
YOU WANT THEM TO WRITE A PARANORMAL ROMANCE THRILLER ABOUT OUR DEATHS?

HELLO, MY LOVELIES!
YOU'RE A PEACH, MARIGOLD.

PSH. MY HOUSEMATES ARE GONE 'TIL FRIDAY. MAKE YOURSELVES AT HOME.
WOW. THIS PLACE HAS THE THING WHERE THE AIR IS COOL!

LOOKS LIKE WE'RE JUST IN TIME FOR THE NOMADS.
FINALLY, ASSHOLES. I'VE BEEN WAITING ALL DAY.
305

HEY!
MAREK!

UH...

WHAT THE HELL ARE YOU DOING?
OH HEH
WELL I JUST THOUGHT HE'D--

BECAUSE
BEARD.

I'VE GOT IT FIGURED OUT. MY MAN DONOVAN IS TRYING TO GET OUT OF HIS LEASE. WE CAN TAKE IT OVER NEXT WEEK.
WE'LL JUST HAVE TO STAY WITH FRIENDS 'TIL THEN.
UGH. DONOVAN.
YOU CAN FINALLY GET INTO HIS BED-ROOM, EVE!
I'M NOT ATTRACTED TO HIM!
IT'S SO SAD HOW YOU GUYS DON'T HAVE A HOME.
WHAT'S SO SAD ABOUT IT?
HOME IS WHERE YOU FIND PEACE. IT'S A NON-JUDGMENTAL SPACE FOR THE WEIRD SHIT YOU DO.
I'D BE SAD TO LOSE THAT, EVEN FOR A DAY.
FUNNY, YOU KEEP PRODDING ME TO MOVE OUT OF MY NON-JUDGMENTAL SPACE.
THAT'S 'CAUSE MINE IS BETTER.
YOU GUYS CAN STAY WITH ME WHENEVER. MY NEIGHBOR'S WI-FI AND CABLE AND TRASH PICK-UP ARE GREAT.
HMPH.
AWW.
THANKS WILL!
HEY, SINCE EVERYONE ELSE IS CRASHING HERE, CAN I--
GET OUT, SEAN.

SO WHEN YOU CROWD GIRLS IN HERE, THEY'RE PRETTY MUCH STUCK KISSING YOU, HUH?
YUP.

MAN, I'VE NEVER LIVED IN MANHATTAN BEFORE. YOU'VE GOT A SWEET SET-UP, JACOB.
IT'LL BE EVEN SWEETER IF EVE EVER COMES BACK WITH THAT ICE.

IS THIS SERIOUSLY A 12-FLOOR WALK-UP?!

JUSTIN WALKS HIS BIKE UP EVERY DAY. YOU STOP THINKING ABOUT IT AFTER A WHILE.
YOU PEOPLE ARE INSANE.

WHATEVER. IT'S NOT LIKE THE PLACE YOU LIVE MATTERS. IT'S ALL ABOUT THE NEIGHBORHOOD.
THAT'S THE PART YOU'RE GONNA CALL YOUR OWN.

UH, JACOB? WHICH FAUCET IS COLD?
THE ONE ON THE LEFT. USUALLY.

NOBODY LOOK AT THE SINK. THAT MAKES THE PLUMBING GO HOT.
GO WHAT?
AAAUGH

YOU NEVER RESPOND TO MY HILARIOUS FWDs, EVEREST. DOES YOUR E-MAIL DO VIDEO?
UH, YEAH... I'M JUST BUSY.
WHY DO YOU STILL HAVE THIS STUPID GEORGE JETSON TOOTH-BRUSH?
I KEEP ALL OF YOUR STUFF IN CASE YOU VISIT!
YOU COULD MOVE BACK HERE FOR A WHILE, YOU KNOW. TO SAVE MONEY.
THAT'S *NOT* GOING TO HAPPEN.
UH... IT'S NOTHING PERSONAL.
REALLY, MOM. IT'S NOT.
SUIT YOURSELF, LITTLE PINBALL.
BUT IT'S NO WONDER YOU'RE NOT COMFORTABLE IN THE PLACES YOU LIVE.
YOU'RE NOT TRULY HOME UNTIL YOU'RE WITH FAMILY.
WHY DOES EVERYONE INSIST ON DEFINING *HOME* TO ME??
MIFF NING! I *RUFF* DEES TANDERINES!
I'LL GIVE YOU A WHOLE BOX OF TANGERINES IF YOU TAKE EVE'S TOOTH-BRUSH OUT TO THE TRASH.
YEFF MA'AM!
WAIT..! COULDN'T WE USE IT TO, LIKE
CLEAN BEHIND THE SINK OR SOMETH
FOOM

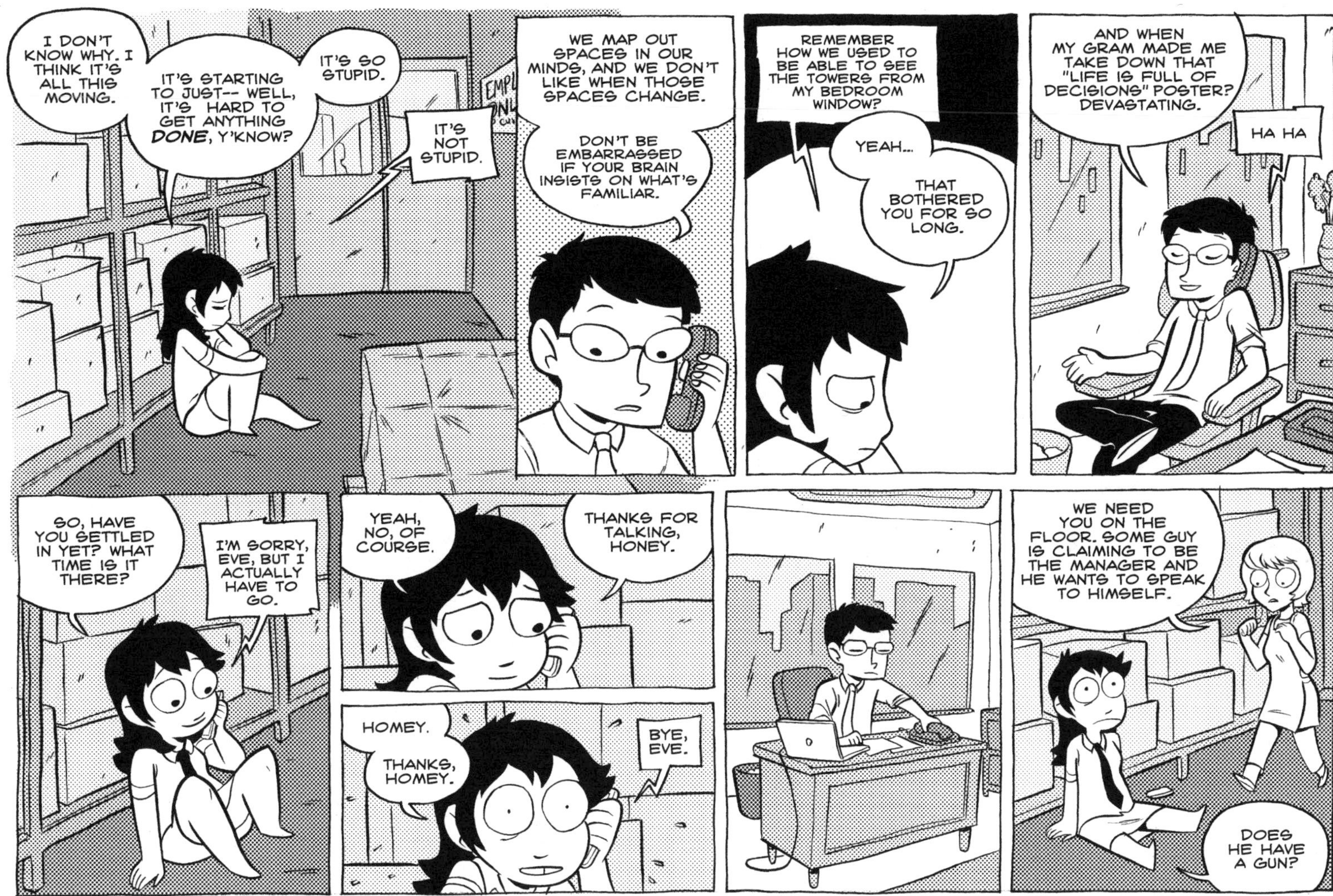
I DON'T KNOW WHY. I THINK IT'S ALL THIS MOVING.
IT'S STARTING TO JUST-- WELL, IT'S HARD TO GET ANYTHING *DONE*, Y'KNOW?
IT'S SO STUPID.
IT'S NOT STUPID.
WE MAP OUT SPACES IN OUR MINDS, AND WE DON'T LIKE WHEN THOSE SPACES CHANGE.
DON'T BE EMBARRASSED IF YOUR BRAIN INSISTS ON WHAT'S FAMILIAR.
REMEMBER HOW WE USED TO BE ABLE TO SEE THE TOWERS FROM MY BEDROOM WINDOW?
YEAH...
THAT BOTHERED YOU FOR SO LONG.
AND WHEN MY GRAM MADE ME TAKE DOWN THAT "LIFE IS FULL OF DECISIONS" POSTER? DEVASTATING.
HA HA
SO, HAVE YOU SETTLED IN YET? WHAT TIME IS IT THERE?
I'M SORRY, EVE, BUT I ACTUALLY HAVE TO GO.
YEAH, NO, OF COURSE.
THANKS FOR TALKING, HONEY.
HOMEY.
THANKS, HOMEY.
BYE, EVE.
WE NEED YOU ON THE FLOOR. SOME GUY IS CLAIMING TO BE THE MANAGER AND HE WANTS TO SPEAK TO HIMSELF.
DOES HE HAVE A GUN?

BZZTBZZTBZZBZZBZZT
BZZT

BZZT

GOT RID OF IT ALREADY?
YEAH...

I ONLY KEPT IT THIS LONG 'CAUSE MARIGOLD LIKED IT.
GUESS IT MAKES ME LOOK DOMESTIC.
IT WILL BE MISSED.

YOU THINK IT'S A GOOD IDEA?

SHAVING YOUR BEARD?
MOVING IN WITH HER.
OH.

I HAVE TO MOVE SOON, EITHER WAY. LIVING WITH MAR' SOUNDS A LOT LIKE TAKING THE NEXT STEP.
AND LIVING ELSE-WHERE--

--AT THIS POINT I CAN'T EVEN EXPLAIN TO HER WHY I'D DO THAT.
I'M LIKE THE WORST PERSON YOU COULD ASK ABOUT THIS, WILL.

YEAH... SORRY.
YOU JUST SEEM TO DEAL WITH BEING IN TRANSITION SO WELL.

DEALING WITH A THING IS SO MUCH EASIER THAN PREPARING FOR IT.
MAN.

THE THREE OF US RAN FROM HOME BECAUSE WE SHARED A DREAM. I *DOUBT* YOU COULD ACT ANY MORE STUPIDLY THAN THAT.
YOU GUYS *ARE* PRETTY RIDICULOUS.
NOT THAT I CAN BLAME YOU.

I'M JUST MORE AWARE OF BEING RECKLESS THAN I USED TO BE.
THINGS ARE COMFORT-ABLE ENOUGH THAT I'D HATE FOR THEM TO CHANGE.
"COMFORTABLE ENOUGH". WHAT A SHINING ENDORSEMENT.

ANY-WAY...

WILL.

DO WHAT YOU THINK IS RIGHT.
YOUR FRIENDS WON'T LET YOU FUCK THINGS UP *TOO* BADLY.

EXCEPT FOR YOUR SLEEP SCHEDULE. THEY'LL LET YOU FUCK *THAT* UP.
SORRY
SORRY

SEE? YES, LITTER BOX!
AND SEE THAT HOLE WHERE THERE'S PROBABLY A MOUSE? YES, MOMMY'S THROWING THAT OUT THERE!
I NEED TO GIVE HER THE KEYS.
WHERE'S HANNA?
SHE'S AT THE DELI.
YOU CAN GIVE THEM TO ME. I'LL BE LIVING HERE, TOO.
TOSS
I GUESS YOU'LL MISS THIS SPACE.
FUCK NO. YOU CAN HAVE THE SPACE.
IT'S THE TIME I'LL MISS.
SLAM!
SO NOT ATTRACTED TO YOU.

IT'LL BE SO GOOD TO HAVE A HOME AGAIN! WE CAN TAKE SHOWERS WITH-OUT SANDALS.
AND DO IT ON OUR *OWN* COUCH!
SO YOU LIKE IT THEN? THE PLACE IS OKAY?
OF COURSE.
I COULD LIVE IN A ONE-ROOM DUMPSTER WITH YOU, AND IT WOULD BE OKAY.
WKXP!
ONLY #1
AH, MAN. THEY'VE GOT THAT SAME STATION OUR DOWNSTAIRS NEIGHBORS USED TO PLAY.
AT ALL HOURS OF THE FUCKING NIGHT!
SIGH.
AT GENTRY CREEK CONDOS, YOU'LL GET SPACE. 1400 SQUARE FEET OF IT. PLUG-INS GALORE, AND A CITY FACING WINDOW!
HOLY COW! HOW IT EVEN POSSIBLE?
...NOT ONLY IS IT POSSIBLE... IT'S BEEN RIGHT UNDER...
...YOUR NOSE.
HAVEN'T I HEARD THIS SOMEWHERE BEFORE?
WAIT A MINUTE, ISN'T THIS--
WE NEED TO MAKE OUT NOW

26

I MET LARRY RIGHT AFTER COLLEGE.
WHEN I WAS DONE WITH COLLEGE, THAT IS.
WITHOUT MONEY OR A PLAN TO GET HOME, I TOOK ANY ODD JOB I COULD FIND.

WE WERE BOTH WORKING AS GUINEA PIGS FOR DIELESS PHARMACEUTICAL. WE GRADUALLY BECAME PLACEBROS.
YOU EVER GO TO CLUB CHUGGIES?

I WAS... KIND OF HURTING FOR FRIENDS.
WHATEVER THAT IS, I WANNA!
AH MAN. YOU'LL LOVE IT.

LARRY SHOWED ME 5,000 WAYS TO MAKE MONEY. IF THERE WAS A GIG IN THE CITY - REGARDLESS OF SAFETY, MORALITY OR FEASIBILITY - HE'D TRIED IT.

NOT TO MENTION THE FUN SHIT WE DID. HE MADE ME LOVE THE CITY AND ITS POSSIBILITIES.
AW DUDE, YOU FLATTER ME!

AT ANY RATE, I'M SO EXCITED WE'RE GONNA LIVE TOGETHER.
TEAM WILLARRY'S BACK IN BUSINESS!
I'M PRETTY INTRIGUED BY THIS NEW PROJECT.

I WISH I WASN'T SO WRAPPED UP IN THE ART OF BAKING. I COULD MAKE MORE MONEY.
MAKING MONEY IS AN ART, GIRL! THAT'S WHAT WILL AND ME ARE FOR.
DUDE! IS THAT TATTOO A SYMBOL FROM THE ANCIENT TSUCHIGUMO TRIBE?

HEH, YEAH! TOTALLY.
GASP! I KNEW A THING!

EVE. HOW ARE YOU?

REALLY FUCKING TIRED.
YEAH...

THIS IS THE ONLY WAY YOU EVER SEE ME! RUNNING ON COFFEE AND HATRED.
YOU SHOULD COME OUT ON FRIDAY. WE CAN TALK ABOUT SOMETHING ELSE.

ANY-THING ELSE.
AND I WILL.

YO EVE!
WE'VE GOT OURSELVES A NEW PERMANENTLY WELCOME GUEST! YOU HEAR?
NO MURDERING THIS ONE.

IT'S SO COOL SEEING YOU GUYS TOGETHER! LIKE REUNITED BROTHERS.
IT KINDA FEELS THAT WAY!

CALL ME IF YOU NEED HELP MOVING, TYCOON.
YOU'RE SWEET. THANKS.

SO MARIGOLD'S OKAY THAT YOU'RE LIVING WITH ME INSTEAD OF HER?
YEAH! SHE UNDER-STANDS YOU NEEDED A ROOMMATE. AND SHE REALLY LIKES YOU!

PERFECT. I'M SO PUMPED.
ME TOO. I'VE BEEN FALLING INTO THE CHASM OF NINE-TO-FIVE LIFE, LATELY.
HA HA. BORING!

HEY, GIMME A SEC. THINK THERE'S A RAZOR BLADE IN MY SHOE.
WILL?

AIMEE? WH-WHAT ARE YOU DOING HERE?!
I LIVE HERE NOW!
WORKIN' AT THE BOOK STORE DOWN THE STREET.
WOW, THIS IS IN DEEP. GOODBYE, BIG TOE MOLE!
YES, DOWN THE STREET! I CONCUR.

DO YOU LIKE THE CITY SO FAR?
IT'S ALL VERY EXCITING! I DON'T HAVE MANY FRIENDS HERE YET.

BUT THERE'S SO MUCH POSSIBILITY, I CAN HARDLY LET IT GET ME DOWN.

ARE YOU STILL WITH UH...
NOT REALLY.

YOU SEEING ANYONE?
NOT REALLY!

YOU AND I BOTH HAVE TROUBLE WITH HONESTY, DON'T WE?
HUH?
WHEW. THAT WAS THE MOST RUST I'VE EVER *SEEN*!

STOP BY THE SHOP SOME TIME, WILL. I'LL BE IN THE NONFICTION SECTION.
YOU NEED ANYTHING SHAVED?

THAT GIRL WAS GORGEOUS. AND TOTALLY INTO YOU!
LARRY, DO YOU THINK I HAVE HONESTY ISSUES?
WHAT? YOU?
YOU'VE ALWAYS COME THROUGH FOR ME, MAN! I'VE **NEVER** SEEN YOU AS DISHONEST.
YOU'RE NOT JUST LYING TO BE NICE, ARE YOU?
WHY WOULD I EVER LIE?
YOU'RE AN HONEST-TO-FUCK GOOD GUY.
NOW, LET'S FOCUS ON THIS INSTRUCTIONAL SCAM ARTIST BOOK.
YOU THINK WE SHOULD HAVE A SECTION ON SUING THE CITY FOR HARASS-MENT?
CONFIDENCE MAN CONFIDENTIAL
I GUESS SO. HAVE YOU ACTUALLY DONE THAT?
NAH, BUT I KNOW OF A FEW GUYS WHO HAVE. WE CAN MENTION THEM.
AND CITE EXAMPLES FROM WIKIPEDIA IF WE GOTTA.
THIS SOUNDS LIKE A LOT OF WORK.

SNAP!

OH MAN. PERFECT SALES PAGE STOCK PHOTO.
NOW WE JUST NEED THE "HAVING AN AMBIGUOUSLY JOVIAL TIME WITH A MULTICULTURAL FRIEND GROUP" SHOT.
OOH. DO WE HAVE A CHAPTER ON DUMPSTER DIVING?!

WE DO NOW! **GET IN THERE!**

SPLOOSH

SNAP
SNAP
SNAP!

WE CAN PHOTOSHOP SOME DOLLAR BILLS IN YOUR HANDS. IT'LL BE SO SICK.
AND GOLD COINS! AND FLAMES!

WELL, ***I'M*** SOBER. LET'S GET OVER TO CHUGGIES.
YEAH. FLAMING DOLLAR BILLS.

YEAH, IT'S DEFINITELY A DREAM OF MINE, INSTRUCTING PEOPLE ON HOW TO INSTRUCT.
YEAH, SHE'S AN ADVERTISING MAJOR!
OH MAN. WE NEED TO BRING KARA OVER HERE.

WE COULD TOTALLY GET YOU LADIES IN ON THIS, YOU KNOW!
THERE'S A LOT OF ADMINISTRATIVE WORK TO DO.
NO SHIT!

GIVE HIM MY NUMBER TOO.
YEAH, WE'RE TOTALLY MOVING INTO AFFILIATE MAR-KETING SOON. WE'LL BE HIRING AND RECRUITING LIKE CRAZY.
WILL HERE IS A FIRM BUT FAIR BOSS. ISN'T THAT RIGHT?

HEH. YEAH. THAT'S... HA HA. THAT'S PROBABLY TRUE!
SO DANG MODEST, TOO!

OH MY GOD. IS THAT TATTOO A REFERENCE TO THE 1959 SCI-FI CLASSIC, THE ANGRY RED PLANET?
YEAH. TOTALLY!

SO ANYWAY, I WAS--

EXCUSE ME, LADIES. MY PARTNER AND I HAVE AN IMPORTANT HEART-TO-HEART SCHEDULED.

DUDE, ARE YOU--
YOU DON'T HAVE TO COME OUT. I'LL BE RIGHT BACK.

...I CAN'T.
I DON'T *WANT* TO BE A PHONY.
YET I'M WRITING THE *BOOK* ON IT.

WE DON'T NEED TO DO THE BOOK. WE CAN DO SOME-THING ELSE.
IT'S NOT THE BOOK, LARRY. IT'S *ALL* OF THE SHIT WE DO.

WHAT WE DO HAS NOTHING TO DO WITH BEIN' PHONY, DUDE.
YOU JUST HAVE TO BELIEVE IN *EVERY*THING YOU SAY!
AND IF SOMETHING ISN'T WORKING, YOU TRY SOME-THING ELSE!

MY MIND DOESN'T WORK THAT WAY.
'CAUSE YOU KEEP IT ALL TO YOUR-SELF?

'CAUSE I--
'CAUSE YOU KEEP IT ALL TO YOURSELF.

MAN, IF I EVER KEPT ANYTHING IN, I'D PROBABLY DIE OF SADNESS.
OR HUNGER.
YEAH, I THINK YOU WOULD.

AND I SAYS TO HIM, DON'T LOOK AT ME -- I ONLY SEE THREE HANDS HERE!
SCOREBOARD
SNKT!
THANK GOD YOU'RE HERE. YOU KNOW YOUR FRIEND CAN WILL HIS OWN REALITY INTO EXISTENCE, RIGHT?
THIS BAR DOESN'T EVEN SERVE OREOS.
DO YOU HAVE A MINUTE?
HEH. COME TO CHALLENGE THIS?
CAN WE TALK OUTSIDE?
WELCOME... TO DIE!
OH. SURE.

SO, GUYS. KARAOKE?

WELL, I TIED UP SOME LOOSE ENDS LAST NIGHT.
NICE! YOU BONED THE CHINESE GIRL?
I TALKED TO HER.
AW.
IT DIDN'T GO VERY WELL.
BUT I FEEL BETTER NOW. LIKE I CAN MOVE FORWARD WITH SOME HONESTY.
THAT'S GREAT.
YEAH. NOW WE CAN FOCUS ON HELPING YOU MAKE RENT!
HAH. NO WORRIES THERE, MAN. MONEY'S NOT AN ISSUE.
I'VE GOT PLENTY OF CASH SAVED AWAY FROM THAT HAWK ATTACK SETTLEMENT.
BUT... YOU SAID YOU NEEDED ME TO MOVE IN. TO PAY THE BILLS!
YEAH, MAN. MY WORDS WERE:
DUDE. YOU **HAVE** TO MOVE IN WITH ME!
DUDE!
I NEVER SAID ANYTHING ABOUT MONEY. BUT THAT'S NICE OF YOU TO CARE.
WHAT'S IMPORTANT IS NOW WE CAN HANG OUT ALL THE TIME! TEAM WILLARRY IS ***REUNITED!***
THANKS FOR BEING MY FRIEND, LARRY.
ANY TIME.
DID YOU WANT CHEX?

27

AUTUMN HAS DESCENDED, AND THE WITCHING HOUR APPROACHES.

AS APPROPRIATE, THERE WILL BE A PARTY.
A HAUNTED HOUSE PARTY!

THERE WILL BE CHEAP BOOZE. UNIRONIC DANCE MUSIC... AND PERHAPS A LITTLE *MURDER!*
I CAN TELL YOU'RE INTRIGUED. AREN'T YOU?

TOO BAD! 'CAUSE YOU'RE NOT INVITED.
HA HA. DID YOU THINK YOU WERE? YIKES.

AH, BUT HERE COME THE GUESTS.

coolitning Going to the fu
anyone riding the bus?
10 minutes ago via txt

marek party.
25 minutes ago via mob

hsthompson RT @Kany
less than a minute ago via txt
hsthompson baking a
also im high
1 minute ago via txt

pugetsean goin
lookin for my ba
pick

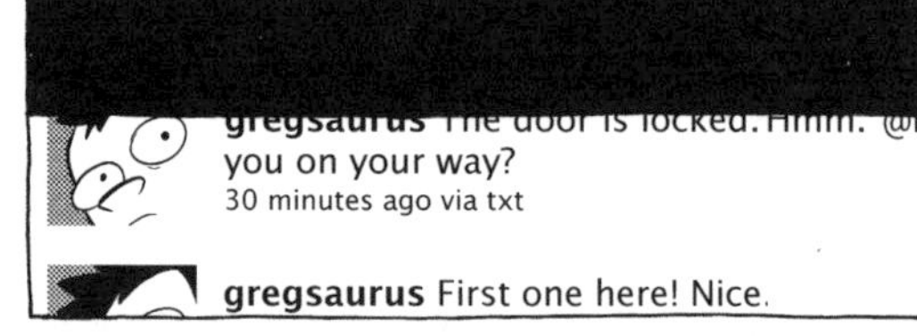
you on your way?
30 minutes ago via txt
gregsaurus First one here! Nice.

goldmar1521 brng
2 gallon jugs.. hope
raise suspicion LOL
2 minutes ago via web
leblanka boss a
hell
1 minute ago via txt
leblanka awwhh
fuck yeah
5 minutes ago via txt

THE PARTY IS STARTING NOW. AND THE FAINT OF HEART WOULD DO BEST TO FLEE IN THE PATH OF...

OCTOPUS DIE

I HOPE YOU WON'T MIND IF I HAVE SOME FRIENDS OVER TONIGHT, MISS MARKS.

OH, NOT AT ALL.

IF IT MAKES IT LOOK MORE LIKE THE MARKS FAMILY ACTUALLY SPENT A NIGHT HERE, IT'S RATHER ENCOURAGED.
WELL, THAT'S MY JOB. YOU WOULDN'T BELIEVE HOW OFTEN THIS IS AN INHERITANCE CLAUSE.
MY LATE ECCENTRIC UNCLE RUTHERFORD WOULD UNDERSTAND. I SIMPLY LACK THE FOUNDATION FOR HIS DEMANDS...
...NO DOUBT WRITTEN IN THE ADVANCED STAGES OF DEMENTIA.
FRANKLY, I CAN'T IMAGINE HOW YOU DO THIS.
IT'S SIMPLE, MA'AM.
I DON'T BELIEVE IN GHOSTS.
SPEAKING OF BEING OVER THE AGE OF EIGHT...
ARE ANY OF YOU ACTUALLY AFRAID OF GHOSTS?
HA HA
HEH
THEN YOU WEENIES WILL BE STAYING IN THE GHOST ROOM. THIRD FLOOR.
WH-WHY'S IT CALLED THAT?
IT WAS INHABITED BY PILFINGTON J. GHOST, NOTED ARCHAEOLOGIST, FROM 1905 TO 1921.
HE WAS DESCENDED FROM GHOSTS!

HEY EVE, WHAT'S YOUR COSTUME SUPPOSED TO BE?

HUH? OH, I'M GRAPES.
HA HA. NICE.
WHAT'S THAT FROM?

WHY DOES EVERYONE KEEP **ASKING** THAT?
IT'S FROM ***GRAPES!***

OH.
...IS THAT, LIKE... A PODCAST?
AUGH!

NOT EVERYTHING IS ***FROM*** SOMETHING!
SLAM!

SQUEEEEEAAAAAAAAAA
EVE?

CRASH
POP POP
POP POP
POP POP
POP POP POP
POP

EVE!
ARE YOU OKAY?
OH MY GOD...
I THINK EVE IS HURT!
SHE'S DEAD, BRO.
YO, IDIOTS! YOU SEEN THE OTHER HALF OF MY OREO?
OH DEAR.
SCREAM
HOW DID THIS HAPPEN?!
I HEARD HER GOING DOWN THE HALL... AND THEN THERE WAS A CRASH. B-BUT I DIDN'T SEE IT!
DID ANYBODY SEE IT?
M
YOU GOTTA ADMIT, THAT'S A PRETTY FUCKIN' BADASS WAY TO GO.
SHE DIED THE WAY I LIVE.

WE HAVE TO STAY CALM. LET'S NOT LET THE UNEXPECTED DEATH OF A FRIEND RUIN THIS NIGHT.
THIS PARTY IS GOING DOWN-HILL **FAST**, LEBLANC!

IF I'M MURDERED TONIGHT, IT'S GOING TO BE **YOUR** FAULT!
M-MURDERED?!
DON'T BLAME ME! YOU'VE BEEN TRYING TO HORN IN ON THIS PARTY FOR **WEEKS**!

ISN'T EVE KIND OF... MOPEY?
MAYBE SHE **JUMPED** OFF THE BALCONY!
Y-YEAH! MAYBE THIS WORLD HELD NO MORE HAPPINESS FOR HER!

YOU CAN BE OPTIMISTIC ALL YOU WANT, BUT IT DOESN'T ADD UP.
EVE WAS ANGRY LAST TIME I SAW HER.
SHE **LOVED** BEING ANGRY.

SAY, WHERE'S GREG?
WHO?

YOU KNOW, THE GUY. WE HANG OUT WITH HIM SOMETIMES.
THAT DOESN'T RING A BELL...
WELL HE'S IN THE HOUSE, TOO.

I GUESS WE... SHOUL TRY TO FI HIM.
SHOULD WE SPLIT UP?!?
NO.

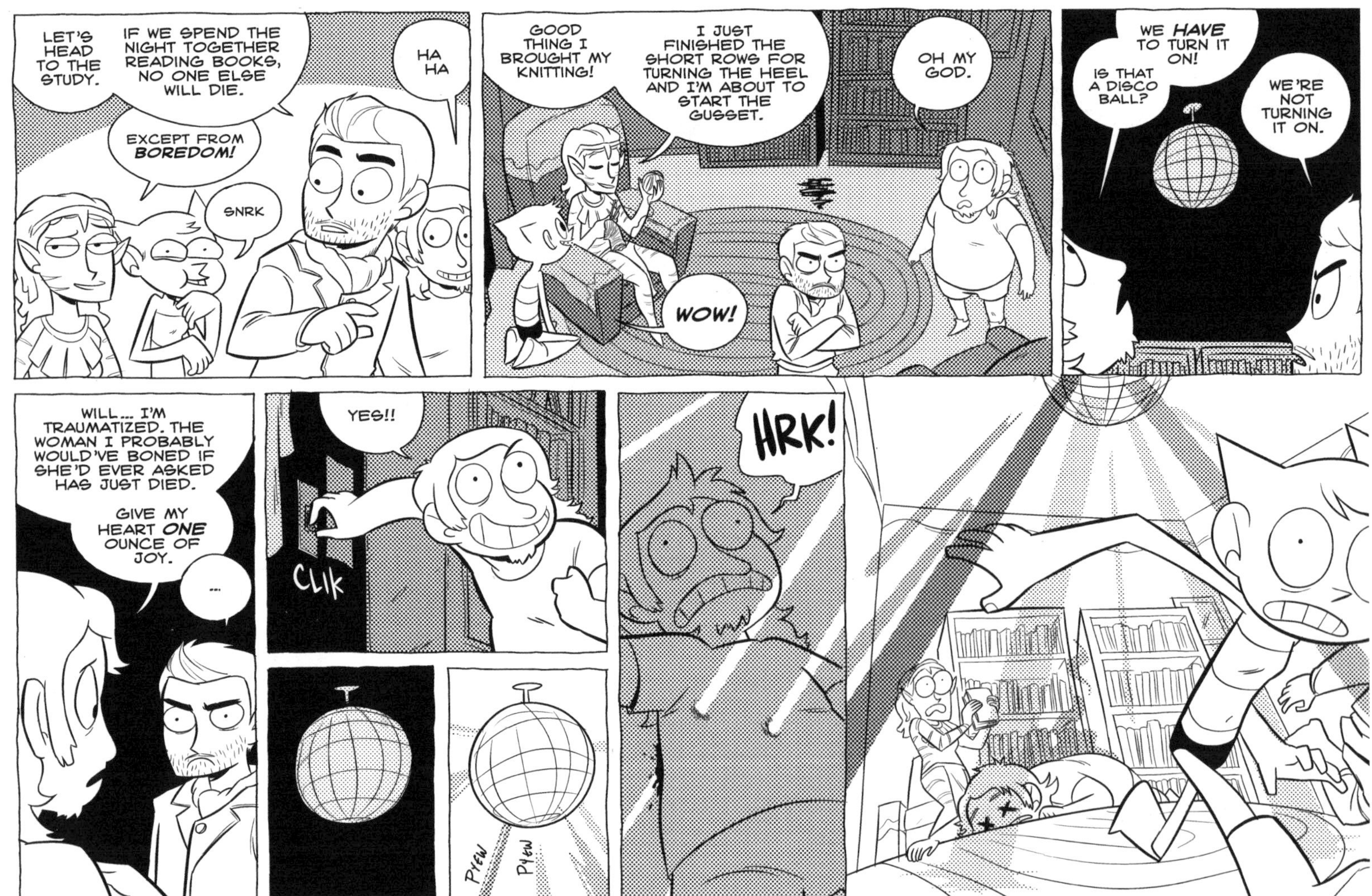
LET'S HEAD TO THE STUDY.
IF WE SPEND THE NIGHT TOGETHER READING BOOKS, NO ONE ELSE WILL DIE.
EXCEPT FROM **BOREDOM!**
SNRK
HA HA
GOOD THING I BROUGHT MY KNITTING!
I JUST FINISHED THE SHORT ROWS FOR TURNING THE HEEL AND I'M ABOUT TO START THE GUSSET.
WOW!
OH MY GOD.
IS THAT A DISCO BALL?
WE **HAVE** TO TURN IT ON!
WE'RE NOT TURNING IT ON.
WILL... I'M TRAUMATIZED. THE WOMAN I PROBABLY WOULD'VE BONED IF SHE'D EVER ASKED HAS JUST DIED.
GIVE MY HEART **ONE** OUNCE OF JOY.
...
YES!!
CLIK
PYEW
PYEW
HRK!

I CAN'T MOPE AROUND. I KNOW EVE WAS MURDERED! AND I'VE GOT TO FIND GREG.
HE'S THE ONLY INKLING OF A CLUE I MIGHT HAVE, TO WHY...

OH EVE! MY ONLY BOARD-CERTIFIED FRIEND. CAN YOU REALLY BE GONE?
UGH, YOU KEPT THAT PIC-TURE?

WH-WHO SAID THAT?!
DUDE! WHY IS EVERYONE IGNORING M--

EVE!!
I NEVER THOUGHT I'D SEE YOU AGAIN!
WHAT THE FUCK IS GOING ON, MAREK?

WE DON'T HAVE MUCH TIME! DO YOU KNOW WHERE GREG IS?
OH, YEAH. I SAW THAT JERK WANDERING AROUND IN HIS STUPID BEAR SUIT.
I CALLED OUT AND HE DIDN'T ANSWER.

HMM. HE MUST NOT BE ABLE TO HEAR YOU IF HE DOESN'T BELIEVE IN GHOSTS.
IS THAT WHAT I AM? A GHOST?

YES... IT'S TRUE. I'M SORRY.
OH, MAN! I WAS AFRAID I MIGHT BE HIGH.

GREG! THERE YOU ARE!
FINALLY!
DO YOU HAVE ANY IDEA WHAT'S GOING--
HM. IT SMELLS LIKE BODIES IN HERE!
I... HAVE TO MUMBLE MUMBLE...
THERE'S A KILLER IN THE HOUSE, GREG! THEY ALREADY GOT EVE.
I CAN'T BELIEVE THEY BUMPED ME OFF FIRST...
WE HAVE TO HIDE OR THEY'LL GET US T--
STATIC..!
OOF!
STOP!
WIMP!

MARIGOLD! DOWN HERE!
HELP ME FIND A LIGHT.
OH, WILL! I NEVER EXPECTED TO DIE AT ALL, LET ALONE TONIGHT.
IT'S THE WORST NIGHT OF MY LIFE!
DON'T TALK LIKE THAT.
THE NIGHT'S NOT OVER YET.
THIS PARTY IS SOMEHOW GOING TO BE *FUN!*
CLIK
IRON MAIDEN
A TORTURE CHAMBER.
NO...

GAH!
SPLOOSH
MARIGOLD, NO!

AAAAAUUGH

THP

PBR..!

AAAHUUG

HE RAN THROUGH HERE... BUT I DON'T KNOW WHICH WAY!
SHIT!

HE WENT DOWN THESE STAIRS.
LET'S GO!
WHOA, WHOA!

THE KILLER GOT YOU, GREG? THAT'S NOT YOU IN THE COSTUME?
YEAH... EVERY-THING WENT BLACK AS SOON AS I ENTERED THE HOUSE.
MY BODY'S IN, LIKE, EVERY KITCHEN CABINET.

I'D TAKE YOU TO SEE IT, BUT IT'S SO DISGUSTINGLY VILE, YOU MIGHT VOMIT YOURSELF TO DEATH.
SO I WASN'T THE FIRST TO DIE!
DID YOU HEAR THAT?

I'M COMING, MARIGOLD!
I'M DEAD.
AGAINST ALL POSSIBLE ODDS THAT OU MIGHT URVIVE UNTIL I'VE TAKEN MY BOOTS--
I'M DEAD.
DEAD.
SO DEAD.

SHUNT

YOU

WHUD
HEY! WHAT ABOUT SAVING ME?

YOU UTTER DICK!
I WAS SUPPOSED TO HAVE AN AWESOME PARTY!
RRRIIPP!!

MISS MARKS?! BUT... WHY?!
THAT'S COUNTESS MARKS TO YOU -- AND ISN'T IT OBVIOUS?

I BOOBY-TRAPPED THIS WHOLE HOUSE, BECAUSE I'M A WOMAN OF DISCERNING TASTES...
...AND I HATE HIPSTERS!

WHAT... DID SHE JUST CALL US?
PARADING ABOUT IN YOUR "WITTY" OUTFITS, REMOVING MEANING FROM ALL THAT'S GENUINE.
I STARTED BY OFFING THE ONES WITH THE MOST INSUFFERABLE COSTUMES!

DROPOUT BEAR WAS THE FIRST TO GO.
SH-SHE THINKS I'M A HIPSTER?

...AND THAT IDIOTIC "FRUIT OF THE LOOM" MASCOT WAS NEXT.
AUUUUGH

DISCO DUCK DIDN'T EVEN OWN A TV, LET ALONE PAY FOR CABLE.
AND COME ON. NOBODY ACTUALLY LIKES AVATAR.
BUT I TELL ALL MY FRIENDS TO SEED THE TORRENTS!
IT'S A REALLY IMPORTANT MOVIE, YOU GUYS.

IN FACT, THE ONLY COSTUME WITH ANY SINCERITY IS THIS WONDERFUL TEEN WOLF! AT LEAST ONE YOUNG MAN APPRECIATES FINE CINEMA.

I'M ACTUALLY SUPPOSED TO BE A WEREWOLF MICHAEL JAC--
RRRRA AAA A

DIE HIPSTER SCUM!

BKAM

PLOK

WHAT THE-- I'M ALIVE!
METAL AS FUCK!

A-A GHOST BULLET?!
THAT MUST BE A REALLY OLD GUN.

GHOSTS!?
AWW, DON'T WORRY... WE'RE FRIEN--
BOO, MOTHERFUCKER!

I THINK I BELIEVE IN GHOSTS NOW.

HAS ANYONE SEEN HANNA?
YO! TURNS OUT I WAS WRONG. THIS ENDED UP BEIN' A GREAT PARTY!

I-IT DID?
YUP! I FOUND A LAPTOP UPSTAIRS.
HAVE YOU GUYS PLAYED MINECRAFT? SHIT'S ADDICTIVE!

MAN, I'M HUNGRY NOW.
I WONDER IF THEY KEEP ANY CEREAL AROUND--

BAAARR

YOUR PARTIES ARE FUCKIN' CLOWN SHOES, LEBLANC.
DON'T THROW ANY MORE. EVER!

COME ON, YOU GHOULS. LET'S HIT THE BARS.
THE GROUNDS-KEEPER WILL LET THE MORTALS OUT IN ABOUT THREE HOURS.
THREE HOURS?!

LEGEND HAS IT THERE'S A REALLY COOL GHOST CANTEEN ON SEVENTH.
DOES THE LEGEND MENTION KAHLUA?
I'LL LEAVE THE POTTERY WHEEL ON, BABE.
GUYS! WAIT FOR ME!

YOU AND I REALLY NEED, LIKE, TWO CONVERSATION POINTS.
I'LL BE UPSTAIRS.

28
Oh! Honey

I DON'T LIKE THE PERSON I AM. I HAVEN'T FOR A WHILE.
USDA ORGANIC
BUT I THINK I CAN BE SOMEONE BETTER.
I JUST... I NEED TO KNOW IF THERE'S ANYTHING BETWEEN US.
'CAUSE IF THERE IS, I THINK IT WOULD BE WORTH CHANGING FOR THAT.
Mets
I'M SORRY, BUT YOU'RE WRONG. IT WOULDN'T BE WORTH IT.
THAT'S NOT WHAT I'M ASKING.
Marigold
"whatevs
Female
21 years
Staten Isl
View More Pics
Last Login:
facebook
Marigold Fuchs
Wall
Info
RECENT ACTIVITY
Marigold is single
10 people like thi
Jesse Von S
fucking kiddi
Monday at 1
Jaclyn Elise
...NO. THERE'S NOTHING BETWEEN US.
FWEEE

CUT IT! DO IT NOW!

ARE YOU SURE ABOUT THIS, MARIGOLD? YOUR HAIR'S GONNA BE SUPER SHORT WITHOUT YOUR DREADS.
REMEMBER HOW LONG YOU SPENT GROWING THEM?
REMEMBER HOW LONG YOUR OLD PAL HANNA SPENT PUTTING THEM IN?
JUST CUT IT, HANNA!

OR I'LL CUT IT MYSELF!

...I DIDN'T MEAN TO UPSET YOU, MAR.
I JUST WANTED TO MAKE SURE YOU'RE SURE.
SOB
...I'M SURE.

WE HAVE TO HELP HER FORGET HIM.

"FORGET" ...WHAT HAPPENED EXACTLY?
SUPPOSEDLY MARIGOLD MADE WILL A SWEATER, AND HE DIDN'T WEAR IT, AND THERE WAS A WHOLE FUCKING FIGHT.

CHRIST. I'VE GOTTEN *INTO* RELATIONSHIPS OVER DISPUTES THAT PETTY.
THIS HAS BEEN BUILDING FOR A WHILE, EVE.

I SAW THE SIGNS. IF ONLY I COULD'VE STOPPED IT FROM ENDING THIS WAY.
I-I REALLY THOUGHT WILL WOULD BE GOOD FOR HER, AND...
HEY, COME ON. YOU CAN'T BLAME *YOURSELF*.

...I MEAN, I FEEL AWFUL TOO. I HOPE WILL'S DOING OKAY.
WILL CAN JUMP IN A *LAKE*.
MARIGOLD'S THE ONE WHO SUFFERS.

YEAH...
CAN YOU HELP ME, THEN? TO GET HER BACK ON TRACK?
OF COURSE. WHAT WOULD CHEER HER UP?

IN TIMES LIKE THESE, NING, THERE IS NO CHEERING UP.
ONLY LOUD, SENSE-ASSAULTING DISTRACTION.
TIMES SQUARE.

CHRISTMAS IS THE ONLY TIME I CAN STAND THIS PLACE.
IT'S STILL A STRESS FACTORY BUT THERE'S A JOY TO THE CHAOS, Y'KNOW?
MM.

UH... YOU HAVE ANY SHOPPING TO DO FOR THE HOLIDAYS?
NO. I MADE GIFTS FOR EVERYONE THIS YEAR.

EH HEH... I DID THAT ONE YEAR. I DUNNO IF PEOPLE APPRECIATED MY FRUITCAKE-FLAVORED BRANDY, THOUGH...

LOVE IS WHEN I LOVE YOU... ONE TWO TIMES, I *HOARD YOU!*
IN MY LIFE WE ALWAYS GO ON...

NEAR, AND FAR... *WHATEEEVER YOU ARE*

BAAAWW!
HEY! HEY BUDDY! CAN YOU PLAY SOMETHING ELSE?

PLEASE. ANYTHING HAPPY.

ALL OF THE SINGLE LADY! ALL OF THE SINGLE LADY!
TK TK
I FUCKING HATE TIMES SQUARE.

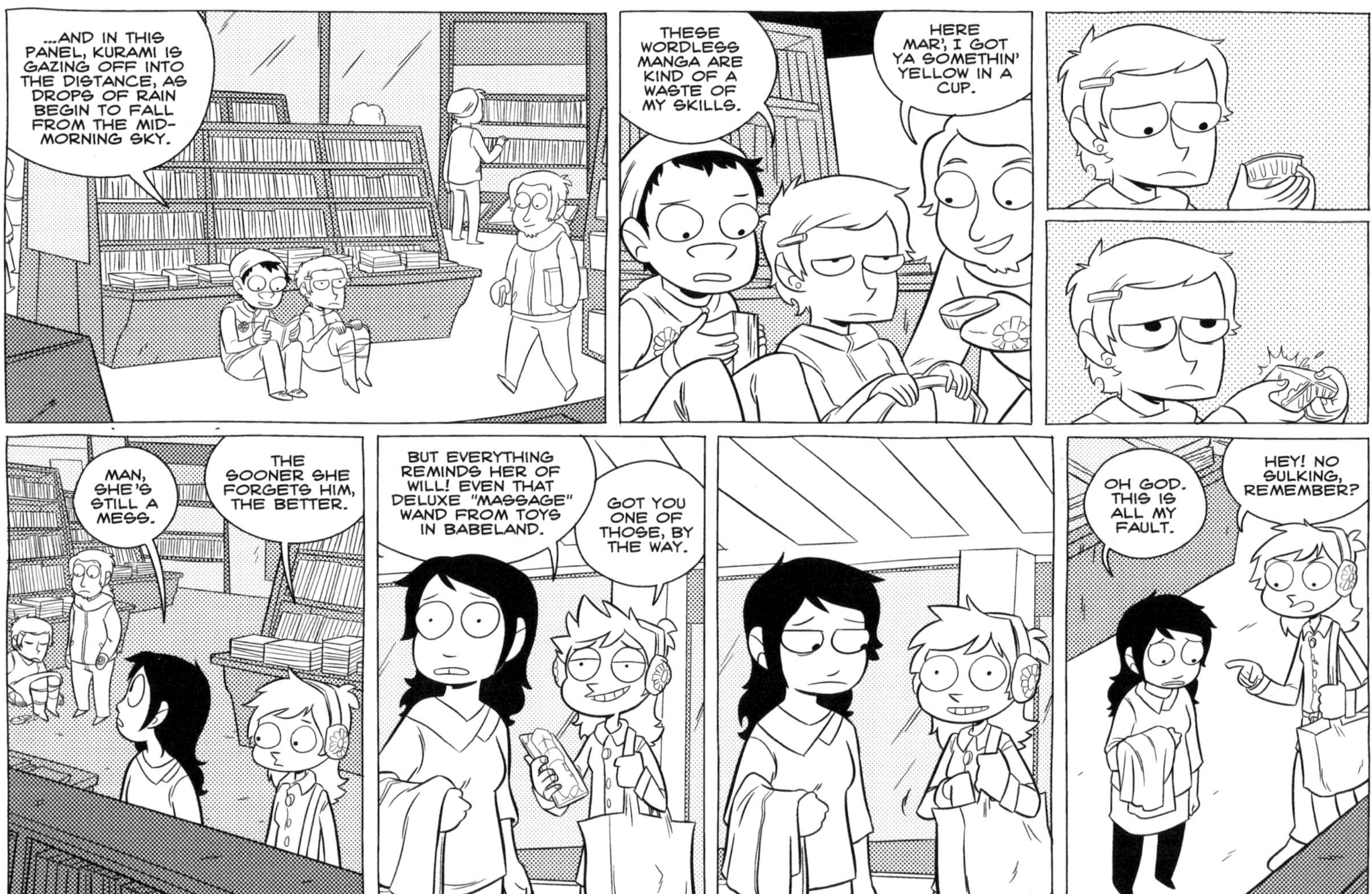
...AND IN THIS PANEL, KURAMI IS GAZING OFF INTO THE DISTANCE, AS DROPS OF RAIN BEGIN TO FALL FROM THE MID-MORNING SKY.
THESE WORDLESS MANGA ARE KIND OF A WASTE OF MY SKILLS.
HERE MAR', I GOT YA SOMETHIN' YELLOW IN A CUP.
MAN, SHE'S STILL A MESS.
THE SOONER SHE FORGETS HIM, THE BETTER.
BUT EVERYTHING REMINDS HER OF WILL! EVEN THAT DELUXE "MASSAGE" WAND FROM TOYS IN BABELAND.
GOT YOU ONE OF THOSE, BY THE WAY.
OH GOD. THIS IS ALL MY FAULT.
HEY! NO SULKING, REMEMBER?

YOU DON'T UNDER-STAND.
YES I *DO!*
WE JUST *HAVE* TO STAY POSITIVE FOR MARIGOLD, UNTIL SHE ...

...RUNS OUT THE DOOR ALL HYSTERICAL-LIKE AGAIN.
MARIGOLD, *WAIT!*

I THOUGHT SHE'D FIND IT USEFUL..!
Microwave Cooking for One
AUGH!

MARIGOLD, WAIT UP! WE CAN'T POWER-WALK THAT INTENSELY!
I DON'T KNOW, GUYS, I...
DON'T YOU WANT TO DO MORE THINGS?
NO... NO MORE THINGS.
C'MON, WE'VE GOT TICKETS TO THE METS VS. THE JETS! HOW OFTEN DOES THAT HAPPEN?
I DON'T EVEN KNOW ANY OF THE SPORTS, AND IT'S GOING TO BE AWESOME!
NOTHING IS GOING TO BE AWESOME!
EVE, I'M NOT LIKE YOU. I DON'T BRUSH THINGS OFF. I CAN'T JUST GET OVER MY PROBLEMS LIKE YOU.
WHAT?
AND HANNA, WHEN'S THE LAST TIME YOU HAD TO WORRY ABOUT WHERE YOU'RE GOING IN LIFE?
OR HOW PRETTY YOU ARE?
THIS IS SO HARD FOR ME. I CAN'T REMEMBER EVER FEELING THIS VULNER-ABLE.
I DON'T WANT ANYONE'S PITY, OR VALIDATION. I DON'T WANT FUN...
BUT--
I JUST WANT TO BE LEFT. ALONE.
DO YOU UNDERSTAND THAT?
I WANT TO BE ALONE.

WE NEVER SHOULD HAVE GOTTEN INVOLVED. IT ONLY MADE THINGS WORSE.
DON'T TELL ME YOU'RE GIVING UP! WE AGREED WE'D **HELP** HER.

DID YOU FORGET ALREADY?
WE TRIED THAT, AND IT WAS A ***DISASTER!***
WE'RE DOING THIS FOR **HER**. WE'VE ***GOT*** TO HELP HER FORGET!

"HELP HER FORGET"... YOU KEEP ***SAYING THAT!***
LIKE A CRYPTIC BROKEN RECORD!

...YOU DON'T UNDERSTAND, NING.

HAVE YOU EVER DONE SOMETHING FOR SOMEONE 'CAUSE YOU LOVED THEM...
AND THEN FOUND YOURSELF RESPONSIBLE FOR IT... ***FOREVER***?
WELL, SURE. I TOOK MY MOM TO BUY THAT STUPID LAPTOP.

WHEN I MET MARIGOLD IN COLLEGE, SHE'D JUST GOTTEN INTO HER FIRST SERIOUS RELATIONSHIP.
AND WHEN IT ENDED... ***BADLY***... I WAS AFRAID SHE'D...
IT WAS SO BAD. I WAS AFRAID SHE'D DO SOMETHING TERRIBLE.

SO I WENT TO AN ALCHEMIST DOWNTOWN. SHE GAVE ME A RECIPE.
CINAMMON AND SALT, STREET PEANUTS, HORNY GOAT WEED...

...JAPANESE LEMON TART, JOY DIVISION'S "CLOSER" IN POWDERED FORM...
HANNA...
...AND THE OPTIONAL BALLPARK BEER. BAKE AT 350° FOR 20 MINUTES.

IT'S CALLED THE BROWNOUT BISCUIT. I DON'T KNOW HOW IT WORKS, BUT IT DOES.
NO...
THE OBJECT OF YOUR DEAREST AFFECTIONS -- FORGOTTEN AS IF A DREAM UPON WAKING.
THIS CAN'T BE REAL!
IT'S REAL.
I TAKE MAR' TO HER FAVORITE CAFE. I BRING HER A PLATE FROM THE COUNTER, WITH THIS ON IT.
AND THEN...
...EVERY TIME, HANNA?
EVERY TIME.
FUCK.
BUT MY HEART CAN'T TAKE IT ANY-MORE. THIS PARTICULAR BREAKUP...
I DON'T WANT TO DITCH WILL, I REALLY DON'T.
BUT HE SCREWED UP. AND MARIGOLD HAS TO BE PROTECTED.
I NEED YOU TO DO IT, NING. I NEED YOU TO GIVE HER THE COOKIE.
THIS IS MADNESS...
YOU SAID YOU FELT RESPONSIBLE FOR THIS.
YOU WANT TO MAKE IT RIGHT, DON'T YOU?

THANK YOU.
HEY... SORRY ABOUT THE OTHER DAY. YOU DIDN'T DO ANYTHING WRONG.
AH, NO... NO WORRIES.
YOU'RE A GOOD FRIEND, EVE. I'M GLAD YOU AND I HAVE GOTTEN--
MARIGOLD, I KISSED WILL.
LIKE... WHEN YOU GUYS FIRST STARTED DATING.
I GOT JEALOUS AND I KISSED HIM.
ON THE MOUTH.

YEAH, I KNOW ABOUT THAT. WILL TOLD ME.

I'M SORRY.
YEAH, WELL... I GOT OVER IT A WHILE AGO.
HE INSISTED IT WAS HIS FAULT.

AND I KNEW YOU GUYS WERE INTO EACH OTHER AT THE TIME.
WHATEVER, RIGHT?
IT'S NOT WHATEVER...

EVE, I'M GOING TO BE FINE.
THERE'S NO HAPPINESS WITHOUT HEARTBREAK. I KNOW THAT.
YOU DON'T NEED TO FEEL RESPONSIBLE FOR WHAT HAPPENED, AND NEITHER DOES HANNA.

I JUST WON'T LET HER SET ME UP WITH HER DUMB FRIENDS ANY-MORE.
SNKT

HERE, LOOK. I MADE YOU A HANUKKAH PRESENT, YOU BOYFRIEND-KISSING BITCH.
MARIGOLD...

...IT'S PERFECT...
YEAH, YEAH. ENJOY.

GOD, I LOVE THIS FLAVOR.
THEY ALWAYS HAVE IT WHEN I NEED IT.

EVE, IS THAT YOU UNDER THERE?
HEY! HA HA. SORRY TO, UH...
IT'S COOL, I JUST CAN'T EVER REALLY HEAR THE INTERCOM, I THOUGHT MAYBE YOU'D BE--
HAHA I WAS DOING MY BEST TO AVOID THE ICE AROUND YOUR STOOP, I WASN'T VERY CLOSE TO THE--
IT'S BEEN A WHILE.
YEAH...
WHAT'S GOING ON?
I JUST, UH...
I J-JUST WANTED TO SAY, I GUESS--

I-I DON'T KNOW THE WHOLE STORY... BUT I DON'T WANT YOU TO BE--
I TOLD YOU YOUR FRIENDS WOULD SUPPORT YOU HOWEVER THIS TURNED OUT, AND...
AND I CAN'T SPEAK FOR THE OTHERS, BUT... Y'KNOW...
AW, NING...
IF NOBODY WANTS TO SEE ME RIGHT NOW, THAT'S ALL RIGHT.
YOU CAN'T TELL PEOPLE WHY THEY SHOULDN'T, OR WEREN'T SUPPOSED TO BE HURT BY THE THINGS YOU'VE DONE.
THERE'S NO TAKING BACK THAT FEELING.
IT'S TAKEN ME A LONG TIME TO UNDERSTAND THAT.
SO, UH...
ME AND LARRY ARE WATCHING TOP GUN, IF YOU WANNA...
NO, NO! HA HA.
THAT'S ALL I CAME TO SAY.
OKAY. WELL LET'S HANG OUT SOON.
YEAH!
SOON!

THIS IS A MANHATTAN-BOUND J TRAIN. THE NEXT STOP IS... FLUSHING AVENUE
MUNCH MUNCH
MUNCH
STAND CLEAR OF THE CLOSING DOORS, PLEASE.

J
METROPOLITAN AVE
CHAMBERS ST MANHTN
YOU'RE SO FULL OF SHIT, HANNA.

29

MAREK.
HAVE YOU SEEN ANYWHERE?
HE'S NOT HERE YET. YOU NEED TO MAKE THE PARTY BETTER, FIRST.
HE'LL COME IF EVERYONE'S ENJOYING THE PARTY.
OKAY.
SEAN AND JULIE KNOW EACH OTHER?
WE CAN'T CROSS THE STREET. IT'S TOO SLUSHY.
THE DANCE FLOOR IS IN THAT BUILDING. MOST PEOPLE WANT TO BE THERE.
OKAY.
FROZEN TOGETHER.
EVERYONE NEEDS TO BE WARMER. I'LL GET SOME COATS.
GET FUR COATS.
20 DOLLARS.
OKAY.

I THINK I GAVE HIM 50 DOLLARS.
MOM. WHAT ARE YOU DOING HERE?
YOU INVITED ME.
YOU WANT ME TO LEAVE?
NO, I--
SHE LEFT, EVE.
NO!
TK
TK
TK
I SENT AN APOLOGY TO HANNA. SHE'LL SHOW IT TO MOM.
IS HERE YET?
YES, FOR A WHILE NOW. HE WENT TO THE KITCHEN.
JACOB, WHERE IS ?
HE WENT OUTSIDE.
DID HE LEAVE?
I DUNNO. MAYBE. HE WENT OUTSIDE A WHILE AGO.
THE SLUSH IS COMING IN THROUGH THE TILES, EVE.
YOU NEED TO SEAL THE CRACKS.

YOU'RE RIGHT.
SORRY, EVERYBODY.
I'LL FIX IT.
HUMMER! FUCK YEAH!
GET THE HUMMER!
SNKT
YOU HAVE TO KEEP DREAMING. DON'T WAKE UP YET.
DON'T LOSE THIS, NING. YOU'RE SO CLOSE TO FIGURING THIS OUT!
YOU WON'T HAVE TIME TO FIGURE IT OUT IN THE MORNING.

30

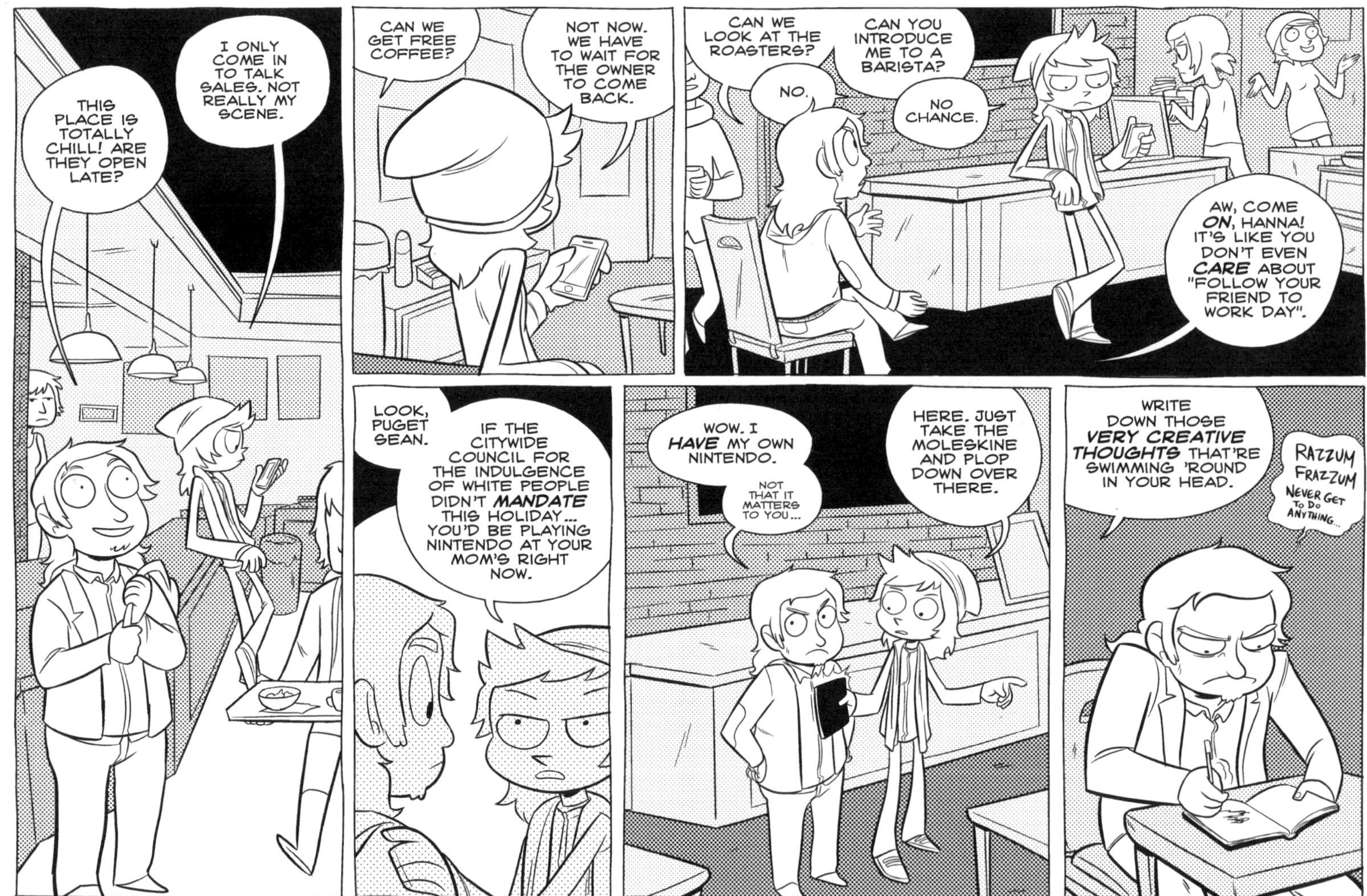
THIS PLACE IS TOTALLY CHILL! ARE THEY OPEN LATE?
I ONLY COME IN TO TALK SALES. NOT REALLY MY SCENE.
CAN WE GET FREE COFFEE?
NOT NOW. WE HAVE TO WAIT FOR THE OWNER TO COME BACK.
CAN WE LOOK AT THE ROASTERS?
NO.
CAN YOU INTRODUCE ME TO A BARISTA?
NO CHANCE.
AW, COME ON, HANNA! IT'S LIKE YOU DON'T EVEN CARE ABOUT "FOLLOW YOUR FRIEND TO WORK DAY".
LOOK, PUGET SEAN.
IF THE CITYWIDE COUNCIL FOR THE INDULGENCE OF WHITE PEOPLE DIDN'T MANDATE THIS HOLIDAY... YOU'D BE PLAYING NINTENDO AT YOUR MOM'S RIGHT NOW.
WOW. I HAVE MY OWN NINTENDO.
NOT THAT IT MATTERS TO YOU...
HERE. JUST TAKE THE MOLESKINE AND PLOP DOWN OVER THERE.
WRITE DOWN THOSE VERY CREATIVE THOUGHTS THAT'RE SWIMMING 'ROUND IN YOUR HEAD.
RAZZUM FRAZZUM
NEVER GET TO DO ANYTHING...

JOE, HI.
OH, HANNA! GLAD YOU COULD MAKE IT.

FIRST OF ALL-- ABOUT THE DEFECTIVE BATCH.
NOTHING LIKE THIS HAS **EVER** HAPPENED BEFORE. I CAN'T **TELL** YOU HOW EMBARRASSED I AM.
HAH! GUESS WE WERE LUCKY, THEN.

NO, HANNA, SEE, I CALLED YOU IN 'CAUSE THE "DEFECTIVE" COOKIES WERE A HUGE HIT!
I NEED YOU TO MAKE MORE.
YOU...

YOU REALIZE THOSE WENT THROUGH THE DIGESTIVE TRACT OF MY HOUSEMATE'S **CAT**, RIGHT?
THE CUSTOMERS DON'T SEEM TO MIND! THEY'RE LITERALLY DEMANDING IT.

HECK, DIDN'T YOU NOTICE THE DEMONSTRATION OUTSIDE?
I GOT MY BUDDY TO PRINT UP T-SHIRTS!
BRING BACK CAT POOP COOKIES
BRING

THIS IS... MY FAVORITE RECIPE, JOE.
WELL, CONSIDER IT IMPROVED. YOU CAN THANK ME LATER.

NEITHER YOU NOR I CAN STALL THIS REVOLUTION!

UH, HANNA. HERE'S YOUR SKETCHBOOK.
Y'KNOW, NO ONE EVER CARES AS MUCH ABOUT YOUR IDEAS AS YOU DO.
NO ONE WHO WANTS TO PAY FOR 'EM, ANYWAY.
I WISH I COULD GO BACK TO THAT, SOMETIMES. WHEN EVERYTHING WAS A SCRIBBLE IN A BOOK.
EVERYTHING WAS A POSSIBILITY.
WAIT HERE.

31

VERMONT SYRUP VILLAGE. THE BEST RESORT IN THE WORLD THAT OWES ME MONEY!
LOOK AT ALL THIS GOD DAMN **SNOW!** SNOW AN' MOUNTAINS AN' SKY!
WELL, HERE WE ARE!
AND WHISKEY. I'M GOING STRAIGHT TO THE LODGE.
PFF. GOOD LUCK FINDING A DRINK THERE.
WHAT? WHY?
THE "LODGE" IS A GIFT SHOP ATTACHED TO A FACTORY. THEY HAVE ***NOTHING.***
TRUST ME, I LOOKED THIS UP.
YOU CAN'T BE SERIOUS.
HEH, NOPE! NO BOOZE FOR MILES.
THAT'S NOT FAIR...
THAT'S NOT FAIR AT ALL!

I'M GONNA GO WATCH CORN GET PRESSED INTO SHAPES. HERE'S THE KEY TO YOUR ROOMS.
COOL.
YOU GOT MAPS AND STUFF? Y'ALRIGHT LOOKING AROUND BY YOUR-SELVES?
...YEAH, WE'RE FINE.
OKAY. YOU GIRLS NEED ANY SPENDING MONEY?
WELL... IT'S BEEN THREE WEEKS SINCE I WAS PAID...
HEH, WELL, ALL RIGHT...
DON'T SPEND IT ALL ON SWEETS!
HEY OLLY. ARE THEY FROM THE CITY TOO?
OH YEAH. CAFE BLASÉ GOT A BATCH OF THAT BAD SYRUP, TOO. WE GOTTA SHARE THE RESORT WITH 'EM.
WOW, CAFE BLASÉ. I'VE BEEN TO THAT PLACE...
BEST COFFEE AND WORST ATTITUDE IN THE WORLD.
C'MON, EVE. BEFORE OLLY REALIZES HE OVERPAID ME.
UH... RIGHT.

OH, SURE, WHY WOULD I WANT A WORKING CHARGER?
GOSH, I PACKED SO MANY DRESSES. YOU THINK JACOB WILL LIKE ME IN THIS ONE?

OH, PLEASE DON'T TELL ME WE'LL BE HEARING ABOUT JACOB ALL WEEKEND.
HMM, YEAH... MAYBE IT'S TOO SLUTTY...

JULIE, WE'RE STUCK IN VERMONT. AND THERE'S A RESORT FULL OF POTENTIALLY INTERESTING PEOPLE STUCK HERE WITH US!
PFFT, LIKE WHO? THE BARISTAS?
LIKE THEY WANNA TALK TO US.

I'M JUST SAYING THIS IS A PERFECT OPPORTUNITY TO EITHER TAKE A CHANCE ON JACOB, OR MEET SOMEONE NEW.

YOU CAN'T JUST BE IN LOVE FOREVER!

BUT IT'S EXCITING, Y'KNOW? NOT KNOWING WHERE IT'S GOING...
WELL, SURE...

BUT IF YOU CHASE THAT ROADRUNNER FOR TOO LONG, EVENTUALLY YOU STARVE.
...OR YOU GET HIT BY A TRUCK, THAT THE ROADRUNNER IS DRIVING.

I DON'T KNOW WHAT ANY OF THAT MEANS.
SORRY, I WAS TRYING SOME-THING.

YO
EVE. IN
HERE.

WOW,
NICE ROOM!
YOU'VE GOT
THIS ALL TO
YOURSELF?
YUP.

JUST
ME N' MY
GUITAR.
UNZIIIIP

OH MY
GOD.
'COURSE,
IT'S NO FUN
ENJOYING
THIS ALL
ALONE.

CARE
TO BE MY
DRINKING
BUDDY,
NING?

JACOB...
I WILL NOT
FORGET
THIS
DEED.
GOOD!
'CAUSE I
NEED A
FAVOR.

SEE THAT
BARISTA?
I'VE *GOT*
TO MEET
HER.
AND?

AND I NEED
YOU TO TELL
HER I RULE.
PFF--
WHAT?

HOW
D'YOU
EXPECT
THAT TO
HELP?

DON'T
YOU KNOW?
SHE'S A
MEMBER
OF THE
GUILD.

THE... GUILD.
IS THAT LIKE SOME NERD SHIT OR SOME-THING?
HA HA
THAT'S CUTE. THERE'S NO NEED TO PLAY DUMB.
I KNOW ALL ABOUT THE GUILD OF THE RISTRETTO.
...AND I KNOW YOU WERE ONCE ONE OF THEM.
YOU'RE DEFINITELY CONFUSED.
REALLY, JACOB. I HAVE NO CLUE WHAT YOU'RE TALKING ABOUT.
GUESS I AM CONFUSED.
FORGET IT.
ANYWAY, I JUST MADE COFFEE. WANT SOME?
...UH, SURE.
GUATEMALA CUP OF EXCELLENCE, FRESH ROASTED THIS MORNING.
IT JUST NEEDS A LITTLE CREAMER...
COFFEE MATE
SUGAR FRE
BROWN SUGAR & HONEY FLAVOR

CAN YOU **BELIEVE** IT'S ONLY FIFTEEN CALORIES **AND** DAIRY FR--
CRAK!!
HH...HHH
HHH... HHHHHH
SO EASY.

GUILD OF THE RISTRETTO. AN ANCIENT ALLIANCE DATING BACK TO THE ADVENT OF THE ESPRESSO ITSELF.
IT'S SAID THOSE TRAINED UNDER THE GUILD CAN PULL THE PERFECT SHOT FROM A HUMAN HEART. THEIR SKILLS ARE RENOWNED ACROSS THE GLOBE, YET THE ORGANIZATION REMAINS A GUARDED SECRET.

GUILD MEMBERS CARRY AN IDENTIFYING MARK THAT IS BOTH DISTINCTIVE AND GENERIC, TO PREVENT OUTSIDER SUSPICION.
GOD DAMN. WHERE DID YOU **HEAR** ALL THIS?

FROM YOU, AT THE COMPANY CHRISTMAS PARTY.
I'M NEVER DRINKING AGAIN.

CAN'T I HAVE JUST ONE DRINK? THIS WOULD SEEM A LOT EASIER.
NOPE. NOT 'TIL YOU'VE MADE CONTACT.

YOU WON'T BE NEEDING IT, ANYWAY.
OOF!

HEY.

SITTING HERE, HUH?

DO YOU KNOW IF, UH... ARE YOU--

EH... THESE BEANS LACK A DISTINCT FLAVOR PROFILE.
NO SHIT!
WHAT'S YOUR NAME? WHERE DO YOU WORK?

I'M EVE-- UH, CATASTROPHE WAITRESS. I'M... BETWEEN JOBS...?
I'M LINE PAINTER JANE.

THAT'S MARY JO, JONATHAN DAVID AND UGLY JACK (HE'S NEW).
DO YOU SKI? YOU SHOULD COME WITH US!
NOT REALLY...
I ACTUALLY WANTED TO ASK...

I'VE KINDA GOT THIS FRIEND OVER THERE WHO WANTS TO MEET YOU, AND...
OH?

HA HA, NO. SORRY, BUT NO.
OH.

WELL THAT'S COOL, UH... I JUST THOUGHT YOU MIGHT
HE HAS BOOZE, JANE.
BOOZE WHAT I NEED!
WHAT?!
I NEED BOOZE TOO!

WHAT SHOULD WE DO?
WHAT IF...
...I JUST ACT NICE TO HIM? WOULD IT BE WRONG TO PLAY WITH HIS FEELINGS?

NOPE! HE'S AN ASSHOLE.
OH.
CAN'T WE JUST BEAT HIM UP, THEN?

TO NEWFOUND FRIENDS!
AND TO SCHEMES.
HEY, JANE? I'D APPRECIATE IF YOU DIDN'T MENTION MY GUILD MEMBERSHIP TO ANYONE.

HATE TALKING SHOP ON VACATION, HUH?
NO PROBLEM.
YOU KNOW IT.

WHAT'S THE REAL REASON? KILLED SOMEONE?
YOU HUSH, TOO. LAST THING I NEED IS TO BE RECOGNIZED.

WHATEVER, I WON'T TELL.
JUST TELL ME WHY!
IT'S JUST...

WHEN YOU LEAVE A GROUP OF ELITES... UNDER ABRUPT CIRCUMSTANCES...
...IT RAISES A LOT OF QUESTIONS.

QUESTIONS THE EXTENT OF WHICH
DEFINITELY DON'T CARE ANYMORE.
YOU THINK JONATHAN HAS A THING FOR JANE? A LONG-HELD NICE GUY BONER?

CHRIST, I DON'T KNOW. WANT ME TO ASK HIM?
YEAH, THAT'D BE GREAT, THANKS!
WHEN DID I BECOME THE FRIENDLIEST PERSON I KNOW?
ALSO CAN YOU ASK HIM WHAT DECADE HE'S TRYING TO MIS-REPRESENT?

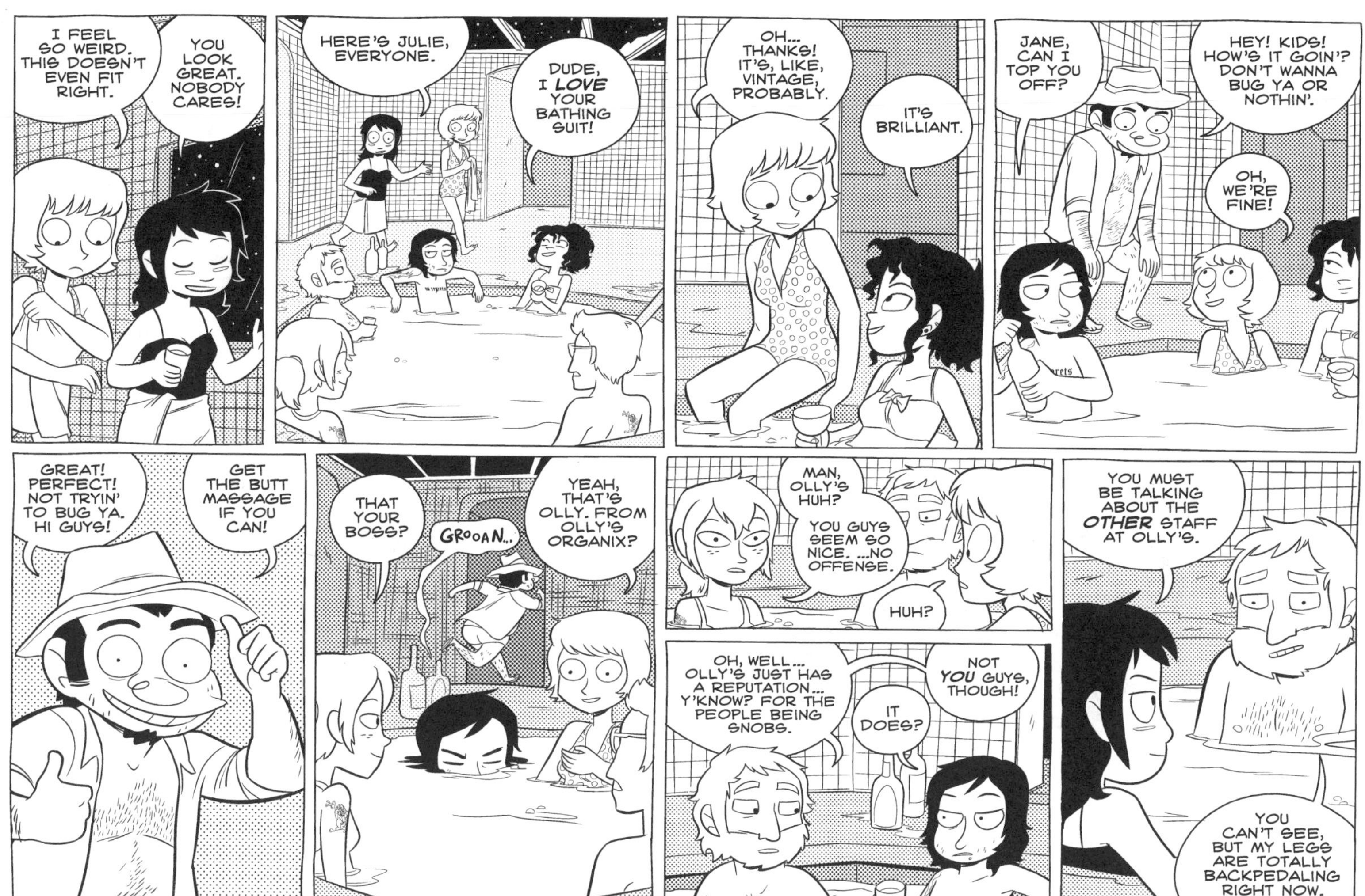
I FEEL SO WEIRD. THIS DOESN'T EVEN FIT RIGHT.
YOU LOOK GREAT. NOBODY CARES!
HERE'S JULIE, EVERYONE.
DUDE, I *LOVE* YOUR BATHING SUIT!
OH... THANKS! IT'S, LIKE, VINTAGE, PROBABLY.
IT'S BRILLIANT.
JANE, CAN I TOP YOU OFF?
HEY! KIDS! HOW'S IT GOIN'? DON'T WANNA BUG YA OR NOTHIN'.
OH, WE'RE FINE!
GREAT! PERFECT! NOT TRYIN' TO BUG YA. HI GUYS!
GET THE BUTT MASSAGE IF YOU CAN!
THAT YOUR BOSS?
GROOAN...
YEAH, THAT'S OLLY. FROM OLLY'S ORGANIX?
MAN, OLLY'S HUH?
YOU GUYS SEEM SO NICE. ...NO OFFENSE.
HUH?
OH, WELL... OLLY'S JUST HAS A REPUTATION... Y'KNOW? FOR THE PEOPLE BEING SNOBS.
IT DOES?
NOT *YOU* GUYS, THOUGH!
no regrets
YOU MUST BE TALKING ABOUT THE *OTHER* STAFF AT OLLY'S.
YOU CAN'T SEE, BUT MY LEGS ARE TOTALLY BACKPEDALING RIGHT NOW.

I FEEL SO DUMB FOR SAYING THAT LAST NIGHT.
PFFT. WHATEVER, JACK.
I'M GLAD YOU WERE AWAKE. I WAS SO HUNGRY!
I DIDN'T MEAN TO BE!
THIS NEW JOB'S MADE ME AN EARLY RISER.
YOU'RE UP ROASTING WITH THE SUN, HUH?
YEAH... BUT I KNEW WHAT I WAS IN FOR WHEN I STARTED. IT'S WORTH IT!
SO YOU LIKE IT?
I DO. THE CAFE'S SUCH A BIG THING FOR ME NOW. MY FRIENDS, MY HABITS...
IT'S A PART OF MY IDENTITY.
WOW! HOW LAME IS THAT?
IT'S NOT! THAT RULES!
ARE YOU SURE YOUVE SNOWBOARDED BEFORE? MAYBE YOU WERE THINKING OF... WALKING?
JUST, UH, KEEP SPOTTING ME.
SLIIIIIDE
IS THAT WHAT I'M DOING? SPOTTING YOU?
WHUMP
HA HA. I CARE SO LITTLE RIGHT NOW.
NEW SPORT. I'M GOING TO PUT THIS ENTIRE MOUNTAIN IN MY POCKET.

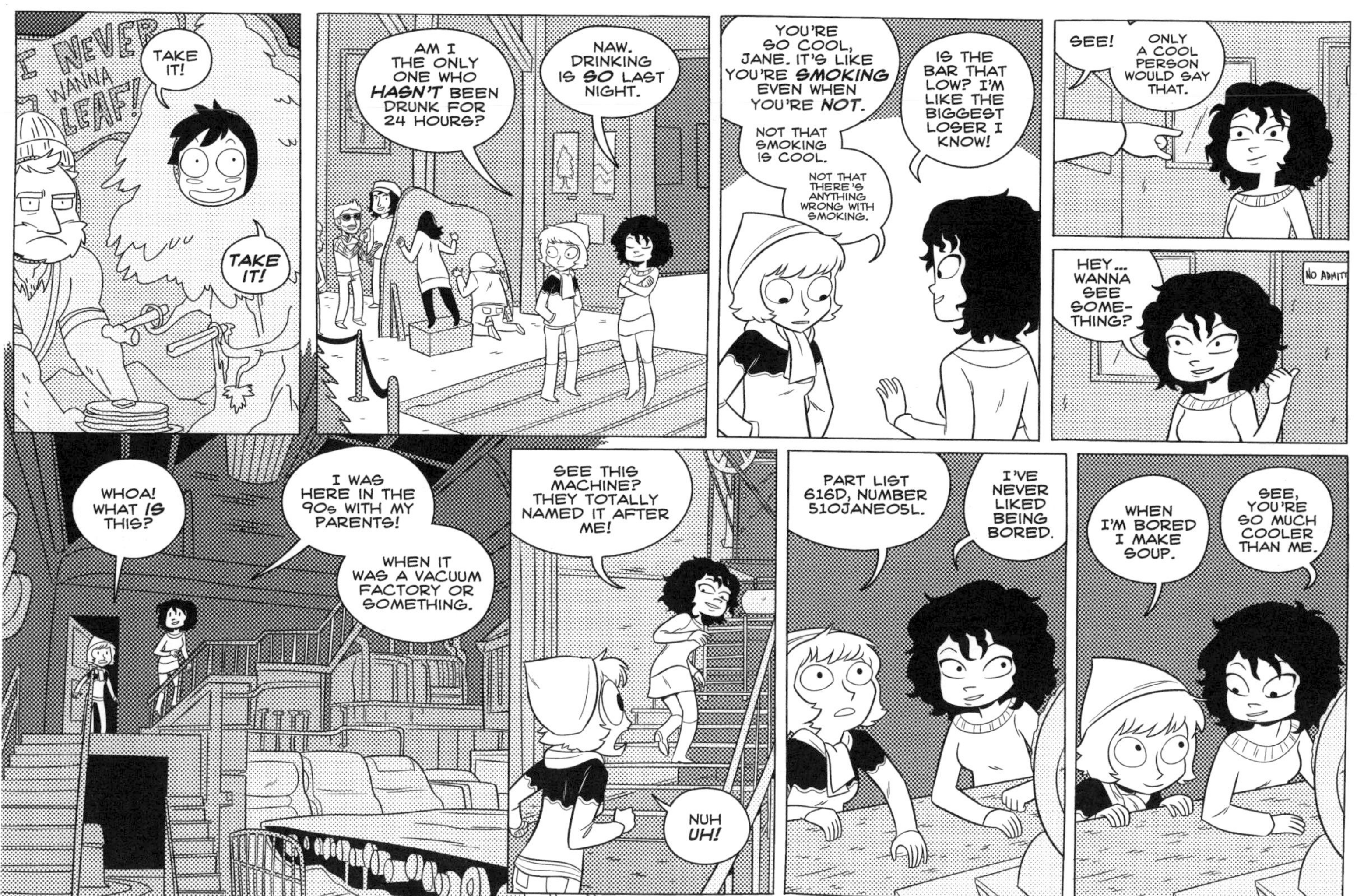
I NEVER WANNA LEAF!
TAKE IT!
TAKE IT!
AM I THE ONLY ONE WHO HASN'T BEEN DRUNK FOR 24 HOURS?
NAW. DRINKING IS SO LAST NIGHT.
YOU'RE SO COOL, JANE. IT'S LIKE YOU'RE SMOKING EVEN WHEN YOU'RE NOT.
NOT THAT SMOKING IS COOL.
NOT THAT THERE'S ANYTHING WRONG WITH SMOKING.
IS THE BAR THAT LOW? I'M LIKE THE BIGGEST LOSER I KNOW!
SEE!
ONLY A COOL PERSON WOULD SAY THAT.
HEY... WANNA SEE SOME-THING?
NO ADMITT
WHOA! WHAT IS THIS?
I WAS HERE IN THE 90s WITH MY PARENTS!
WHEN IT WAS A VACUUM FACTORY OR SOMETHING.
SEE THIS MACHINE? THEY TOTALLY NAMED IT AFTER ME!
NUH UH!
PART LIST 616D, NUMBER 510JANE05L.
I'VE NEVER LIKED BEING BORED.
WHEN I'M BORED I MAKE SOUP.
SEE, YOU'RE SO MUCH COOLER THAN ME.

LAST NIGHT HERE, GUYS. MAKE EVERY MOMENT COUNT!
IN A MINUTE.
YOU LOOK UNEASY, JONATHAN.
I COULD SWEAR I'VE MET THAT GIRL BEFORE THIS TRIP.
YOU'VE PROBABLY SEEN HER AROUND BROOKLYN.
MAYBE. BUT THE RECOGNITION SHAKES ME TO MY CORE.
LIKE REALIZING YOUR DENTIST IS ACTUALLY A TAXIDERMIST.
THAT'S IT. SHE STUFFED MY GRANDMA'S CAT!
NAH... EVE'S OKAY.
I'M NOT TRYING TO BE ACRIMONIOUS, JACK.
JUST REMEMBER. TRUST IS THE PERMISSION YOU GIVE FOR OTHERS TO HURT YOU.
HERTZ... HAVE I RENTED A CAR FROM HER?
THAT'S THE REASON ANY OF US JOINED THIS GUILD.
PROTECTING THE KEYSTONE OF THE RISTRETTO IS MY FIRST PRIORITY.
RIGHT ON.
RITE AID. SHE'S THE FOUNDER OF RITE AID.
FOR ALL WE KNOW.

OH YEAH, ALMOST ALL HOTELS HAVE IT. JUST ROUND THE SIDE.
NO NEED TO THANK ME.
DUDE!
GOOD COFFEE
WELL, THANK YOU.
I'M SO GLAD I GOT TO MEET YOU, JULIE.
YEAH, ME TOO!
IT'S CRAZY. WE'VE PROBABLY CROSSED PATHS A MILLION TIMES.
I KNOW.
BUT IT HURTS TOO MUCH TO THINK ABOUT THAT.
THE THING IS... I'M IN LOVE, JANE.
SO LONG AS I THINK I HAVE A CHANCE WITH JACOB, I'M GONNA HOLD OUT FOR THAT.
OH.
I... GUESS I CAN UNDERSTAND THAT.
MAYBE.
WITH GREAT CONCENTRATION.
WELL, NO BIG DEAL, ALRIGHT?
I'M GETTING A DRINK. WHAT DO YOU WANT?
I'M NOT SURE AT THE MOMENT.

IS JULIE LEAVING ALREADY?
'SCUSE ME, NING, I JUST SAW JANE.

JACOB, WAIT.

JANE'S ONLY BEEN USING YOU FOR YOUR BOOZE. SO HAVE I.
YOU SHOULD KNOW THAT.
UH HUH. AND?

AND... THAT'S THE **WORST**, RIGHT?
DOESN'T IT UPSET YOU?

OH, NING. I'M **USED** TO BEING USED BY GIRLS.
IN FACT, I RATHER **ENJOY** IT.
BUT..!

I CAN'T BELIEVE I'M EVEN SAYING THIS...
YOU'VE GOT A **LOT** GOING ON. YOU CAN FIND SOME-ONE WHO LIKES YOU WITHOUT TRICKS OR BLACKMAIL.

YEAH, BUT NOT SOMEONE I WANT.
SO IT GOES.

YOU CAN'T **PAY** FOR ADVICE THIS GOOD!
NO... NOT WHEN YOU'RE GIVING IT AWAY.

I HAVE A CONFESSION.
WHEN I FIRST SAW YOU GUYS, I HAD TO FIGHT THE NOTION THAT YOU WERE AWFUL.
AWFUL?

YOU KNOW. FULL OF YOUR-SELVES, LAZY, ENTITLED...
UNFRIENDLY.
HA HA. WE DESERVE IT FOR THINKING THE SAME OF YOU.

MAYBE WE'RE ALL UNFRIENDLY.
OR MAYBE NONE OF US ARE. ...OR MEAN TO BE.
PEOPLE ARE SHY, OR THEY DON'T KNOW WHAT TO SAY, OR...

THEY'RE AFRAID OF SOUNDING DUMB.
YEAH!
YEAH.

GOD, WE'RE ALL SO AFRAID OF PEOPLE NOTICING OUR ACTUAL FAILINGS...
...MAYBE WE LIKE TO FANTASIZE THERE'S SOME WEIRD ELITIST ARCHETYPE JUDGING US FOR NO GOOD REASON.

LIKE WE NEED SOMEONE TO BE THAT MUCH MORE SELF-CONSCIOUS THAN US.
I THINK I DO.

TP

YOU SAID THE CAFE GAVE YOU AN IDENTITY...
THAT GIVES YOU GUTS, DOESN'T IT?
YES.

I NEED THAT AGAIN.
TO SAY WHAT I MEAN WITHOUT...

AW, WELL, SAYING WHAT YOU MEAN... THAT'S NOT SO--
I REALLY LIKE YOU.
YEAH?
YEAH. AND IT TOOK ME THIS ENTIRE BUILDUP TO SAY SO.
WELL I LIKE YOU TOO!
I MEAN IT'S BEEN FUN HANGING OUT AND DOING STUFF...
...AND I WASN'T SURE IF I SHOULD SAY ANYTHING OR IF...
HA HA. WHAT?
OH RIGHT.
WE'RE STILL TALKING ABOUT IT.
GOD DAMN.

PAW PAW
7:31
SHIT.
I HAVE TO GO PACK.
'KAY.
203

LATE NIGHT, NING?

LET ME GUESS... YOU WERE TUNING HIS *GUITAR!*
W-WHAT?
YOU AND JACOB... I'M SUCH AN *IDIOT* FOR NOT SEEING IT...
THIS IS WHY YOU TRIED TO KEEP ME AWAY FROM HIM!

JULIE, WAIT. LET ME EXPLAIN.
I DON'T *NEED* YOUR EXPLANATION!

SLAM!

ACTUALLY, YEAH, WHY DON'T YOU EXPLAIN.
I WAS WITH JACK, NOT JACOB.

OH!
WOW, I'M GLAD I WAITED FOR YOU TO SAY THAT.

KNOCK KNOC

VERMONT GUILDSMEN.
ALL SEVEN OF THEM.
CATASTROPHE WAITRESS. MEMBER 437, BROOKLYN CHAPTER.
MISSING AND UNACCOUNTED FOR SINCE CREMA-TORIUM SEVEN.
MIKE VAN MONTPELIER, FAIR TRADE SPECIALIST. WE MET IN '05...
...THOUGH I WOULDN'T EXPECT YOU TO REMEM-BER.
A LOT OF PEOPLE PUT THEIR TRUST IN YOU.
WITH YOU WE SHARED OUR MOST INTIMATE SECRETS, BECAUSE YOU WERE *ONE OF* US.
DO YOU KNOW HOW DELICATE THAT SORT OF TRUST CAN BE?
YES. I DO.
THEN THE GUILD WANTS DISCLOSURE.
TELL US WHERE YOU WENT.

ALL RIGHT.
HERE'S WHAT HAPPENED.
SO BASICALLY I QUIT MY JOB BECAUSE I WAS SORT OF THINKING OF GOING BACK TO SCHOOL, AND ALSO THE HOURS WERE KICKING MY ASS;
AND I WAS SEEING THIS GUY KIND OF, NOT REALLY, BUT HE WAS TELLING ME THERE MIGHT BE AN OPENING AT *HIS* WORK, AND THEN *THAT* DIDN'T PAN OUT,
AND I WAS WAITING TO HEAR BACK FROM THE COLLEGE -- I MEAN I HADN'T APPLIED, BUT I'D CONTACTED THEM WITH SOME QUESTIONS -- AND THEN I DECIDED THERE WAS NO POINT IN GOING BACK, AND...
AND, Y'KNOW...
HOUSING BUBBLE... AND THE REPUBLICANS...
...AND... THE G TRAIN?
WE'VE ALL BEEN THERE, EVE.
WOW... IF I'D'VE KNOWN SOONER...
THANK YOU FOR BEING CANDID WITH US TODAY.

JANE!

WERE YOU GONNA LEAVE WITHOUT SAYING GOODBYE?
I WAS GOING TO TRY.

WELL, YOU FAILED.

...BUT I'M GLAD YOU TRY.

BYE, JANE.
HEY... TELL EVE I'M SORRY FOR WHAT HAPPENED.

GOD DAMN IF THE PEOPLE I LOVE DON'T EMBARRASS ME SOMETIMES.

SO, EVE...
NOW THAT EVERYTHING'S OKAY WITH THE BARISTAS, ARE YOU GONNA SEE JACK AGAIN?
FUCK *HIM!* STATUS-OBSESSED PRICK.
JUST 'CAUSE EVERYONE'S APPROACHABLE DOESN'T MEAN THEY'RE *WORTH* TALKING TO.

WALLING THEMSELVES UP IN THEIR COOL FUCKING FORT OF SECRECY...
AS IF THERE'S ANYTHING TO GUARD.
ISN'T THERE?

YOU WANT TO KNOW THE KEYSTONE OF THE RISTRETTO, JACOB?
YES.
OKAY.
FINE GRIND, LIGHT TAMP, SLOW EXTRACTION.
PERFECT SHOT.
WHAT? I COULD'VE GOOGLED THAT IN ABOUT FIVE SECONDS!
YEAH, WELL, SECRETS MEANT A LOT MORE BEFORE THE INTERNET.
YOU KIDS ALL READY? NO RUSH OR NOTHIN'...
JUST MAKIN' A SNOW BRO.
WANNA JOIN US, OLLY?
AWW, NAH...
I MEAN, YOU SEEM TO BE DOIN' FINE WITH IT. BUT IF YOU NEEDED AN EXTRA MAN, I COULD PROBABLY...
WE COULD REALLY USE YOUR HELP, OLLY.
OKAY!
HOPE YOU KIDS GOT SOME REST!
NEXT WEEK AT THE SHOP IS GONNA BE HELL.

32

OH DUDE, PASS IT DOWN!
YEAH MAN, LET'S HAVE 'EM.
I'M TOTES HUNGRY YO!
LARRY MY BRO, CAN WE PLAY SOME TUNES?
OF COURSE!
HELL YEAH!! THIS IS MY JAM.
LOOKS LIKE YOU'RE ALL SET UP DOWN HERE.

ISN'T IT THE BEST?
IT'S SO COOL OF THE LANDLORD TO LET YOU USE THE DOWNSTAIRS.

WILL, YOU HAVE NO IDEA.
SINCE I WAS BORN I'VE LIVED IN APARTMENTS...

ALL MY LIFE I'VE WANTED A BASEMENT FULL OF BUDDIES.

WELL, I'M OFF TO ATLANTA ON BUSINESS!
WOO! HOTLANTA!
YOU GUYS HELP YOURSELVES TO WHATEVER YOU WANT, OKAY?
ASK WILL IF YOU NEED ANYTHING.
YEAH!
HOTLANTAAA!
WoOo!
BYE, BUDDIES.
LATER...
DID LARRY FORGET HIS PHONE?
YEAH, I TEXTED HIM ABOUT THAT.
SHOOT! SHOOT THE TREE!
YOU BUDDIES ARE DUMB.
HEY MAN, YOU HAVE ANY MORE CHIPS?
WHERE'S LARRY?

I'M BACK!
AAAND THERE'S MY PHONE. CAN'T BELIEVE I LEFT IT!

MESSAGE... RECEIVED... THREE DAYS AGO.
HEY LARRY MY BRO. UH, WHAT'S UP!

NOT AN EMERGENCY OR ANYTHING, BUT THE DORITOS ARE TOTALLY CASHED.
CAN YOU PICK SOME UP WHEN-- BEEP!!

MESSAGE... RECEIVED... TWO DAYS AGO.
YO MAN, YOU GET MY LAST MESSAGE? NO BIG DEAL, JUST PRETTY HUNGRY DOWN HERE...

MESSAGE... RECEIVED... YESTERDAY.

UH, HEY MAN, SORRY TO UH, BUT THE SITUATION IS GETTING UH
MESSAGE... RECEIVED... YESTERDAY.
BRO WE'RE WICKED STARVED

THE BUDDIES ARE DEAD.
OH, FUCK!
I WAS SUPPOSED TO FEED THEM.
GEEZ. I'M SUCH A DOUCHE.
WOW.
I'M SORRY MAN.
SIGH... IT'S ALL RIGHT.
I'LL PICK UP SOME MORE BUDDIES ON MY WAY HOME FROM WORK, OKAY?
WELL... IF YOU WANNA...

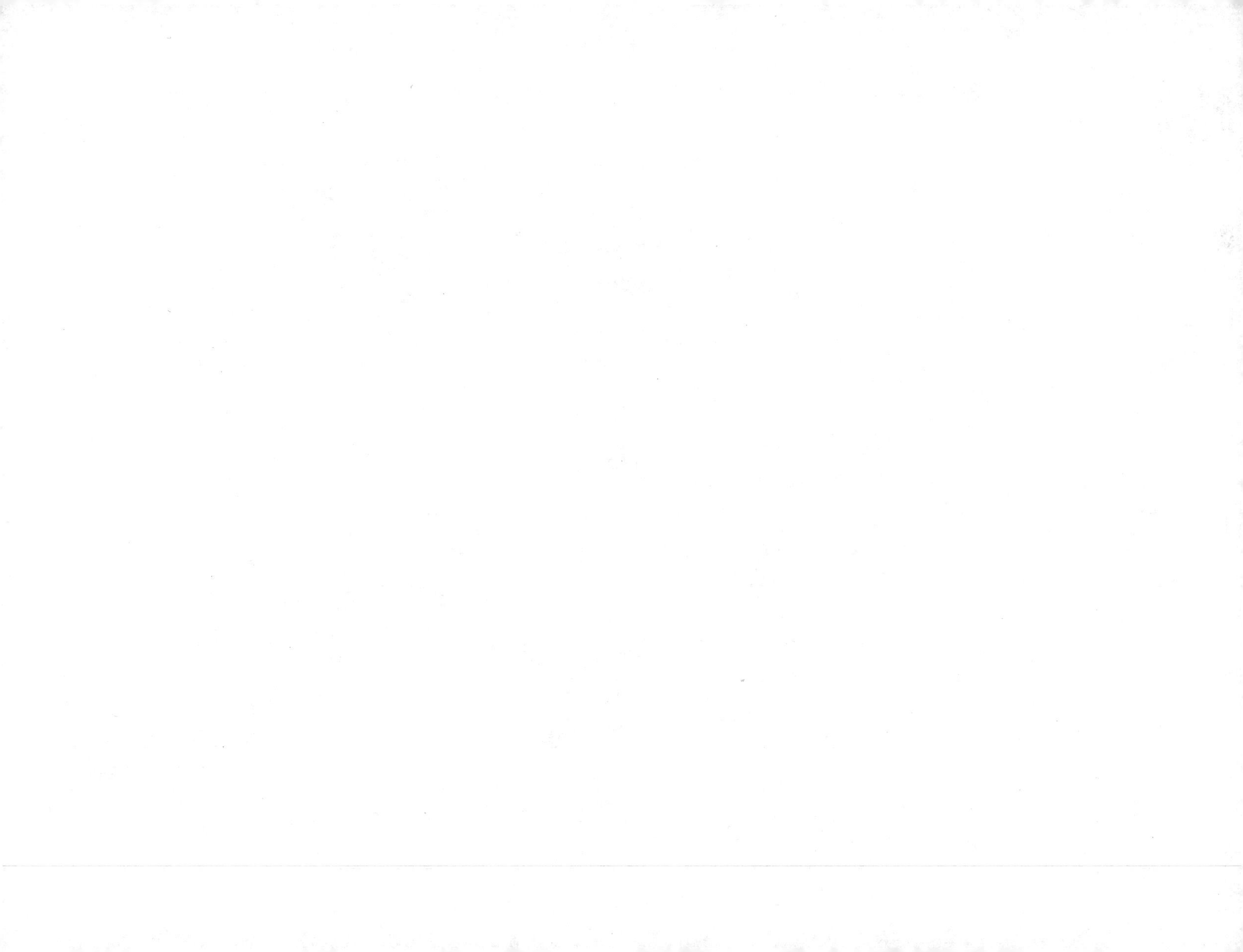

33

GOD DAMN. WHAT A GREAT DAY OFF THAT WAS. NEW YORK IN THE SPRING, AM I RIGHT?
RENT
OLLY'S ORGANIX
FOR RENT
CAFES, OUTDOOR MARKETS, BOUTIQUE BROWSING... FOR A CHANGE I FEEL RESTED!
GOOD FOR YOU.
NO SMALL MIS-COMMUNICATIONS RESULTING IN A LIFETIME OF REGRET?
NOPE!
HEY, SPORT. HOW WAS YOUR WEEKEND?
UH... OLLY JUST FIRED ME.
WHAT?!
WHY?
H-HE SAID IT'S NOTHING I DID... HE JUST CAN'T AFFORD TO...
OH, NO...
YOU WANT THE CLEAN CONSOLATION, OR THE KIND WITH THE SWEARS?
SOME SWEARS WOULD BE NICE...

I KNEW THINGS WERE GETTING BAD... I JUST DIDN'T THINK IT'D BE SO ABRUPT.
ME NEITHER.

WILL YOU BE OKAY?
I THINK SO.
I WAS GONNA MOVE OUT NEXT MONTH, BUT... I GUESS I CAN STAY WITH MY FOLKS A LITTLE LONGER.

I'M SO SORRY, JULIE. I'LL REALLY MISS YOU.
AW, WELL... I'LL STILL BE AROUND.
OLLY'S OFFERED ME AN INTERNSHIP.

AN INTERNSHIP... HERE?!
YEAH, Y'KNOW? IT MIGHT LEAD TO SOMETHING.

OH GOD... WHO TOLD OLLY WHAT AN INTERN IS?
DID I LEAVE THE NEW YORK TIMES ON HIS DESK?
I-I THOUGHT YOU'D BE HAPPY!

NO, JULIE.
THIS IS VERY GRAVE NEWS.
YOU MUST RUN.

...AND... GET YOU COFFEE?
RUN!!!

...AND SHE SEEMS PERFECTLY OKAY WITH IT! LIKE IT'S SOME FOREGONE CONCLUSION!
UGH!
WAIT. IS THAT HOW THE STORY BEGINS?
OOPS. NO.
JULIE WAS FIRED AND REHIRED AS AN INTERN.
HM.
BUT INTERNSHIPS ARE **GREAT**, EVE!
I'VE MADE INVALUABLE **CONNECTIONS** AT THE BAGEL FACTORY.
MY RECORD STORE INTERNSHIP'S BEEN WORTH IT FOR THE EXPOSURE ALONE.
I COULDN'T **LIVE** WITHOUT MY INTERNSHIP AT THE CLINIC FOR INJURED BEES. I'M KINDA SURPRISED **YOU** DON'T HAVE ONE, EVE.
ARE YOU PEOPLE **SERIOUS?**
WHAT ABOUT A **SALARY?**
I INTERN AT NBC'S "THE SALARY." THE WHOLE CREW COMPETES TO WIN A **PAYCHECK!**
AAAUGH!
GET OUT OF MY HOUSE, YOU SERFS!
HELPFULISTS!
PAYLOADERS!
B-BUT WE DIDN'T LET **ELIJAH** IN YET!
ELIJAH CAN GET HIS ***OWN DAMN WINE!***
DANG.

IT'S LIKE AN INTERNSHIP IS THIS WAY OF **PRETENDING** TO HAVE A CAREER.
AND THESE BUSINESSES... WOULD IT KILL THEM TO PAY PEOPLE?
PROBABLY. YEAH.
OH, **COME** ON!
NING, THERE'S NOTHING WRONG WITH OFFERING INTANGIBLES FOR WORK.
EVEN **CHRIST** HAD INTERNS.
I WORKED UNDER MY MENTOR, JACQUES PEPPERONI, FOR OVER TWO YEARS! HE TAUGHT ME THE ESSENTIAL PRINCIPLES OF WASHING HIS PANS, ARRANGING HIS KNIVES AND WALKING HIS WIFE'S DOG!
OF COURSE... I'D NEVER TAKE ON INTERNS. MY ONE ATTEMPT WAS KIND OF A DISASTER.
THERE YOU GO.
SO WHAT'LL YOU DO? CONVINCE JULIE TO QUIT?
THERE'LL BE FIFTY M.F.A. GRADS IN LINE FOR HER JOB.
NO... I HAVE TO TALK TO OLLY. MAKE HIM UNDERSTAND.
UNDER... STAND...
OH! YOU MEAN **TRICK** HIM!
RIGHT.

EVE THINKS IT'S A BAD IDEA... BUT I DON'T HAVE **ANY** PROSPECTS.
AND IT MEANS SO MUCH TO MY PARENTS THAT I HAVE **SOME** KIND OF JOB.
GOSH... I. DON'T KNOW WHY I'M **TELLING** YOU ALL THIS!
'CAUSE I **ASKED**?
OH, YES.
AREN'T YOU A VETERINARY STUDENT? HOW DOES UNPACKING FROZEN MEAT HELP YOUR CAREER?
...I GET TO WORK WITH ANIMALS.
WHY NOT WORK AT A SHELTER? AT LEAST THERE'S NO PRETENSE, THERE.
A SHELTER... T-THAT'S BRILLIANT! YOU'RE SO SMART.
YOU'RE SMART **TOO**, YOU IDIOT. YOU JUST DON'T STAND UP FOR YOURSELF!
JUICER IS ALL PLUNGED, JANE.
OH, JULIE. THIS IS CAFE BLASE'S NEW INTERN, LOUISE.
HEY! I **KNOW** YOU!
FAMOUS... PHOTOGRAPH BEING IN... PERSON!
IS THIS LIKE A PUBLICITY STUNT?
IT'S LIKE A WORKING FOR HALF OF THE TIP JAR STUNT.
OH! SORRY.
AS IF BEING FAMOUS PAYS THE BILLS.
IF A CANDID VAGINAL SELF-PORTRAITIST CAN'T MAKE A LIVING, WHAT HOPE IS THERE FOR THE **REST** OF US?

HOW CAN THIS BE? NO ONE'S EVER DEFEATED THE CASH WIZARD!
WE DID IT... WITH A LITTLE HELP FROM CAPITALISM!
LET'S ALL GO HOME.
AND THAT'S WHY YOU SHOULD CUT COSTS AND REHIRE JULIE!
HAVE YOU BEEN TAKING NOTES, OLLY?
NICE OF YOU TO TRY CHEERING ME UP, NING.
BUT BETWEEN YOU AND ME...
I'VE FAKED A LOT OF NUMBERS IN MY TIME, AND THESE NUMBERS ARE UNFAKEABLE.
SO THIS IS WHY JULIE WAS...
IF SOMEONE DOESN'T PICK UP THE SLACK, THE STORE CLOSES.

JULIE!
WHAT'RE YOU DOING HERE?
HI JACOB. JUST PICKING UP SOME THINGS...
...HEY, I'M SORRY ABOUT WHAT HAPPENED... AND STUFF.
IT'S, Y'KNOW... NOT THE SAME WITHOUT YOU.
I MISS YOU GUYS.
BUT I FEEL GOOD ABOUT THIS... Y'KNOW? IT'S GOOD FOR ME.
MAN, THAT'S GREAT. YOU'RE SO DRIVEN...
YOU'LL FIND SOMETHING THAT MAKES YOU HAPPY.
JULIE! HOW'S IT GOING?
YO! INTERN!
WHY CAN'T I SEE MY REFLECTION IN THOSE BANANAS?!
ON IT!
YIKES.
IT'S FINE. IN SIX MINUTES I'M HIS BOSS AGAIN.

EVE! IS THIS A GOOD TIME?
UH, YEAH! I'VE GOT TWO HOURS OFF. GONNA ENJOY THE FLEETING SPRING.
I JUST WANTED TO TELL YOU... I QUIT MY INTERNSHIP.
OH! REALLY?
AND IT'S 'CAUSE OF WHAT YOU SAID THE OTHER NIGHT.
SCENTED OIL
BATH SOAPS
I SPEND SO MUCH TIME LOOKING THE PART OF MY DREAM LIFE... AND NOT ENOUGH TIME BUILDING IT.
I WANT TO WORK TOWARD SOMETHING BETTER.
WOW! WELL, GOOD FOR YOU, MARIGOLD!
COFFEE
OUT OF BUSINESS
GOD, I WAS SO FIRED UP TODAY, I EVEN CONVINCED MY HOUSEMATES TO QUIT THEIR UNPAID JOBS!
I WANNA BE A TOUGH-LOVE FRIEND LIKE YOU, EVE.
CLOSED
cutesy's vintag
REC
SORRY
TIMES ARE TOO TOUGH TO DWELL ON OUR PETTY WANTS.
CLOSED
PRETTY SOON WE'LL ALL START DEMANDING WHAT WE'RE WORTH.

CLOSED
FOR RENT
I'VE GOT A GOOD FEELING ABOUT THE FUTURE.

34

SO WHO DO YOU KNOW HERE, UH...?
WILL. I LIVE HERE.
WHAT?
I'M LARRY'S ROOMMATE.
OH! GOTCHA!
SORRY, YOU'RE LIKE THE ONLY PERSON I DON'T RECOGNIZE.
LARRY HAS A LOT OF FRIENDS.
WHAT?

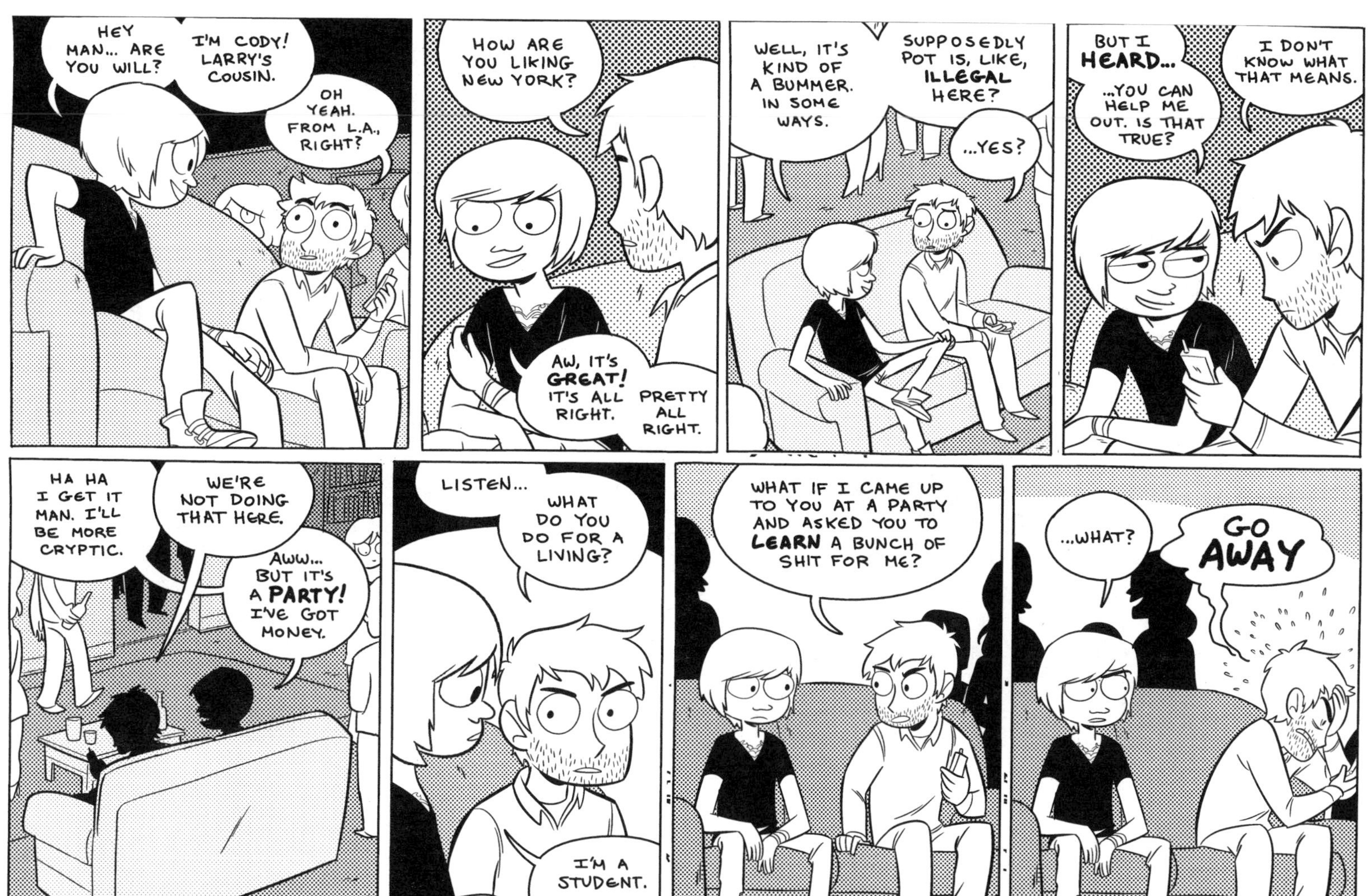
HEY MAN... ARE YOU WILL?
I'M CODY! LARRY'S COUSIN.
OH YEAH. FROM L.A., RIGHT?
HOW ARE YOU LIKING NEW YORK?
AW, IT'S GREAT! IT'S ALL RIGHT.
PRETTY ALL RIGHT.
WELL, IT'S KIND OF A BUMMER. IN SOME WAYS.
SUPPOSEDLY POT IS, LIKE, ILLEGAL HERE?
...YES?
BUT I HEARD...
...YOU CAN HELP ME OUT. IS THAT TRUE?
I DON'T KNOW WHAT THAT MEANS.
HA HA I GET IT MAN. I'LL BE MORE CRYPTIC.
WE'RE NOT DOING THAT HERE.
AWW... BUT IT'S A PARTY! I'VE GOT MONEY.
LISTEN...
WHAT DO YOU DO FOR A LIVING?
I'M A STUDENT.
WHAT IF I CAME UP TO YOU AT A PARTY AND ASKED YOU TO LEARN A BUNCH OF SHIT FOR ME?
...WHAT?
GO AWAY

AND THEN I SAYS TO HER... WHOSE CROSS-SECTION OF A CONVERSATION ACTUALLY SOUNDS LIKE THIS?
PFFF!
HEY!
SORRY TO GET HERE SO LATE.
NO, NO!
FAR AS I'M CONCERNED, THINGS'VE JUST STARTED.
WHO'S YOUR FRIEND?

TO MAKE UP FOR HOW LATE I AM, I'M TOTALLY GONNA CLING TO YOU AND **REFUSE** TO MINGLE ON MY OWN.
HA HA. THAT'S FINE.
TECHNICALLY YOU'RE EARLY.
YOU'RE THE ONLY ONE I INVITED WHO CAME.
SERIOUSLY?
BUNCH OF JERKS.
WELL, WHO DO YOU LIVE WITH? I WANNA MEET **SOME**ONE, DAMN IT.
OH, UH--
LARRY. PARTY WAS MY BRAIN-CHILD.
COOLEST DUDE HERE, PLEASED TO MEET YA.
OH WOW. YOU TWO **MUST** BE BROTHERS.
CLOSE ENOUGH.
CAN I GET YOU ANYTHING? FLOWERS? ADORNMENTS? PEDESTALS?
AH, NO THANKS. I'M DRIVING.
SHE'S FUNNY!
SHE'S **SO** FUNNY.

SORRY.
THEY CAN BE... INTENSE.
IT'S COOL. THIS IS LIKE THE FIRST TIME I'VE SEEN ANYONE OUTSIDE OF WORK IN **WEEKS**.
THAT'S SO HARD TO BELIEVE. **YOU?**
FUCK OFF! I CAN BE A SAD SACK.
I MOVED HERE FOR MY BOY-FRIEND...
THINGS FELL APART ALMOST INSTANTLY.
I DIDN'T EVEN MIND.
I WAS CONVINCED I HAD A MILLION OTHER REASONS TO BE IN NEW YORK.
WOULDN'T ANYONE?
BUT YOU DON'T END UP SEEING ALL THOSE PEOPLE YOU KNOW IN A CITY.
NO...
THEY'VE ALREADY GOT LIVES.
I WAS SO GOOD AT MAKING FRIENDS IN A SMALL TOWN. HERE... NOT AT ALL.
AW HEY, IT'LL GET EASIER...
IT DOESN'T FEEL RIGHT.
IT'S LIKE STANDING BEHIND THE DOOR OF A CROWDED ROOM...
HEARING THE WARM RUMBLE OF VOICES...
SO NEAR, YET IN A COMPLETELY SEPARATE WORLD.
THAT SOUNDS **AMAZING** RIGHT NOW.
YEAH.

THIS IS ALL I WANT RIGHT NOW.
YEAH?
WELL, MAYBE NOT ALL...
KNOCK KNOCK
UH... WILL? IT'S CODY...
HEY, UM...
WHAT AM I ABOUT TO WITNESS...?

WHAT IS IT.
SORRY TO BOTHER YOU, MAN...
JUST... THERE'S A GIRL HERE. UPSTAIRS.
SHE'S LOOKING ALL OVER FOR YOU.
SHE SAID SHE COULDN'T STAY LONG, SO, Y'KNOW... THOUGHT I SHOULD TELL YOU.
YEAH.
THANKS, CODY.
I HAVE TO GO SAY HI TO SOME-ONE.
IS THAT OKAY?
MUST BE IMPORTANT.
TRUST ME.
THERE'S NO PLACE ON EARTH I WANT TO LEAVE LESS.

WADDUP, DUMMY?
IT'S GOOD TO SEE YOU.
YEAH.
I STARTED TO MISS YOUR SKETCHY ASS.
SO... HOW'S MAR'?
FINE. SHE'S FINE.
WASN'T AT FIRST... BUT, Y'KNOW... LIFE AND THE EARTH'S ROTATION AND SHIT.
I HANDLED THAT ALL WRONG. I FEEL SO STUPID NOW.
ARE WE DOING THAT?
DON'T APOLOGIZE TO ME.
WE'VE BEEN THROUGH MUCH DUMBER STUFF THAN THIS.
BESIDES, THE GUY I'VE BEEN BUYING FROM IS RUBBISH.
OF COURSE HE IS.

YOU WANT?
AH, NO THANKS...
LISTEN, HANNA. I'VE BEEN THINKING A LOT ABOUT THIS...
I WANT TO START COOKING AGAIN.
TAKING IT SERIOUSLY.
UH HUH.
I KNOW YOUR BUSINESS HEAD TO TOE. I CAN HELP YOU IF YOU TEACH ME.
I WOULDN'T EXPECT ANY-THING ELSE. I JUST WANT TO--
I GET IT. YEAH.
I'LL THINK ABOUT IT.
OKAY.

WELL, I SHOULD GET GOING. JUST WANTED TO SEE YA.
AW, ALL RIGHT...

BESIDES, YOU GOTTA HURRY BACK TO WHOEVER'S IN YOUR ROOM.
HA HA... YEAH RIGHT.
I WAS JUST ABOUT TO SLEEP.

YOU WILL NEVER
BE ABLE
TO LIE TO ME.

CHRP
OKAY, MY EYES ARE RESTED! LET'S--
FUCK.
CHRP
CHRP
YOU SHOULD'VE WOKEN ME...
AWW. YOU LOOKED SO TIRED.
SIGH. WHEN DID I GET SO LAME?
STILL...
IT WAS THE BEST NIGHT I'VE HAD IN AGES.
THAT'S PRETTY SAD.
OH FUCK YOU!

MAKIN' EGGS, HUH?
BATH-ROOM'S, UH...
DOWN THERE.
YOUR GIRL HATES ME, DUDE.
FOR BOTHERIN' YOU LAST NIGHT.
ACTUALLY, CODY, ABOUT THAT...
YOU HANDLED SOMETHING DELICATE WITH FINESSE. THAT WAS VERY IMPRESSIVE!
HERE-- IT'S FROM MY OWN SUPPLY.
BUT... THE PARTY'S OVER.
WHAT AM I SUPPOSED TO DO... FLY HOME WITH THIS?
YOU'RE NOT VERY GOOD AT PARTIES, MAN.
HEY, CODY.
HOW MANY PASSED-OUT IDIOTS ARE ON MY FLOOR?
I DUNNO, TWELVE? FIFTEEN?
WHY?
YOU'RE ALL GETTING CROISSANTS.
OH WORD?!

35

SO YOU SAID YOU WERE A WRITER? FOR WHAT EXACTLY?

TV MAINLY. I DO A LOT OF ADAPTATION TREATMENTS.
AH COOL! WOW!
NO CLUE WHAT THAT IS.

THEY'RE OUTLINES OF OTHER PEOPLE'S STORIES. I ANALYZE AND WRAP THEM INTO NICE LITTLE TV PACKAGES.
MAN.

I WANTED TO BE A WRITER, KIND OF... YEARS AND YEARS AGO. THAT MUST BE SO GREAT.

WHAT ARE YOU, THIRTY-FIVE? YOU'RE TALKIN' LIKE YOUR LIFE'S OVER.
HA HA NAH, I JUST--

Y'KNOW. I'VE JUST BEEN FOCUSING ON OTHER THINGS.
SURE.
LIKE WHAT?

I DON'T EXPECT PEOPLE TO ASK WHEN I SAY STUFF LIKE THAT.
OH.
DID I MAKE YOU NER-VOUS?

KINDA. BUT NOW IT FEELS LIKE THE ANSWER'S IMPORTANT.
AWW. I'M JUST JERKIN' YOUR CHAIN OFF.

BUT YEAH... BY THEN THE CUSTOMERS WERE RIOTING, AND MY WHOLE BODY WAS COVERED IN PEAS, SO...
HA HA

YOUR LIFE'S A SITCOM, EVE NING. A FARCE IN THREE ACTS.
HA HA. SURE.

SO WRITE A SCRIPT ABOUT ME.
I'M COMPLETELY SERIOUS. YOU'RE THE HERO, I MIGHT ADD.

I WOULD... BUT I CAN'T SELL YOU AS A WOMAN OF COLOR. WE GOTTA CHANGE THAT PART.
EH HEH... RIGHT.

IT'S FUNNY BECAUSE IT SUCKS.
I HEAR THAT A LOT.

ANYWAY, EVE, I SEE NOTHING ROMANTIC HERE. LET'S JUST BE TRIVIA NIGHT BROS, OKAY?
OH!

WELL THAT'S A RELIEF! ME NEITHER! HA HA.
WOULDN'T WANT OUR TRIVIA TO SUFFER.
I'MA HAVE A SMOKE

HEY...

WHAT IF...
WE JUST GAVE THIS A TRY? I MEAN...

MAYBE THERE'S NOTHING NOW, BUT... I FEEL LIKE THERE **COULD** BE SOMETHING.

YOU'RE A GREAT HERO, EVE, DON'T GET ME WRONG.
YOU'RE CUTE, SYMPATHETIC... YOUR NAME'S AN AMUSINGLY CRUEL PUN...

AN AMUSINGLY CRUEL **WHAT?**

BUT I'M THE TROUBLE-SOME FRIEND...
AND THE PROTAGONIST NEVER DATES THE TROUBLESOME FRIEND.

WHO WOULD EVEN **SHIP** US?
I'M SHIPPING US!

DON'T BE UPSET...
WHAT DO YOU **SEE** IN ME?

I DON'T KNOW, I...
IT SEEMS LIKE YOU **KNOW** ME. YOU SEE ME BETTER THAN **I** DO.

I CAN'T HELP YOU FIND YOUR WAY. I SEE A HERO WITHOUT DIRECTION.
STOP **CALLING** ME THAT!

I DON'T **WANT** TO BE THE HERO!
I DON'T WANT SOME KIND OF CONGRUOUS NARRATIVE!
I DON'T WANT PEOPLE TO IDENTIFY WITH ME, OR EVEN PAY **ATTENTION** TO ME!

YEAH...
THERE'S JUST NO STORY IN WHAT YOU **DON'T** WANT.

THIS WAS FUN! CALL ME WHEN YOU'RE ANYTHING BUT HORNY, 'KAY?

COOL.

ANOTHER TROUBLE-SOME FRIEND.

36

KNOCK KNOCK!

HANNA!
YOU GET A **JOB** YET, YOU OBAMA-LOVING TRUST FUND HIPPIE FUCK?

WHAT A NICE SURPRISE.
I JUST MADE YOU A FEW THINGS. I WAS LOSING **SLEEP** IMAGINING WHAT YOU'VE BEEN EATING.

DON'T DESTROY the AMERICAN DREAM

EVE! MARIGOLD!
HEY DUDE.
CUTE TENT, MAREK.

THANKS! IT'S NOT IDEAL FOR THE WEATHER, BUT...
...BUT NEITHER IS LIVIN' IN THE MIDDLE OF **WALL STREET** FOR THREE WEEKS.

AW, IT'S JUST GONNA MAKE YOU WANT HIM **MORE,** HANNA.
YEAH. WE CAN WAIT OUT HERE IF YOU GOT **URGES.**
OH MY GOD SHUT UP ALL OF YOU.

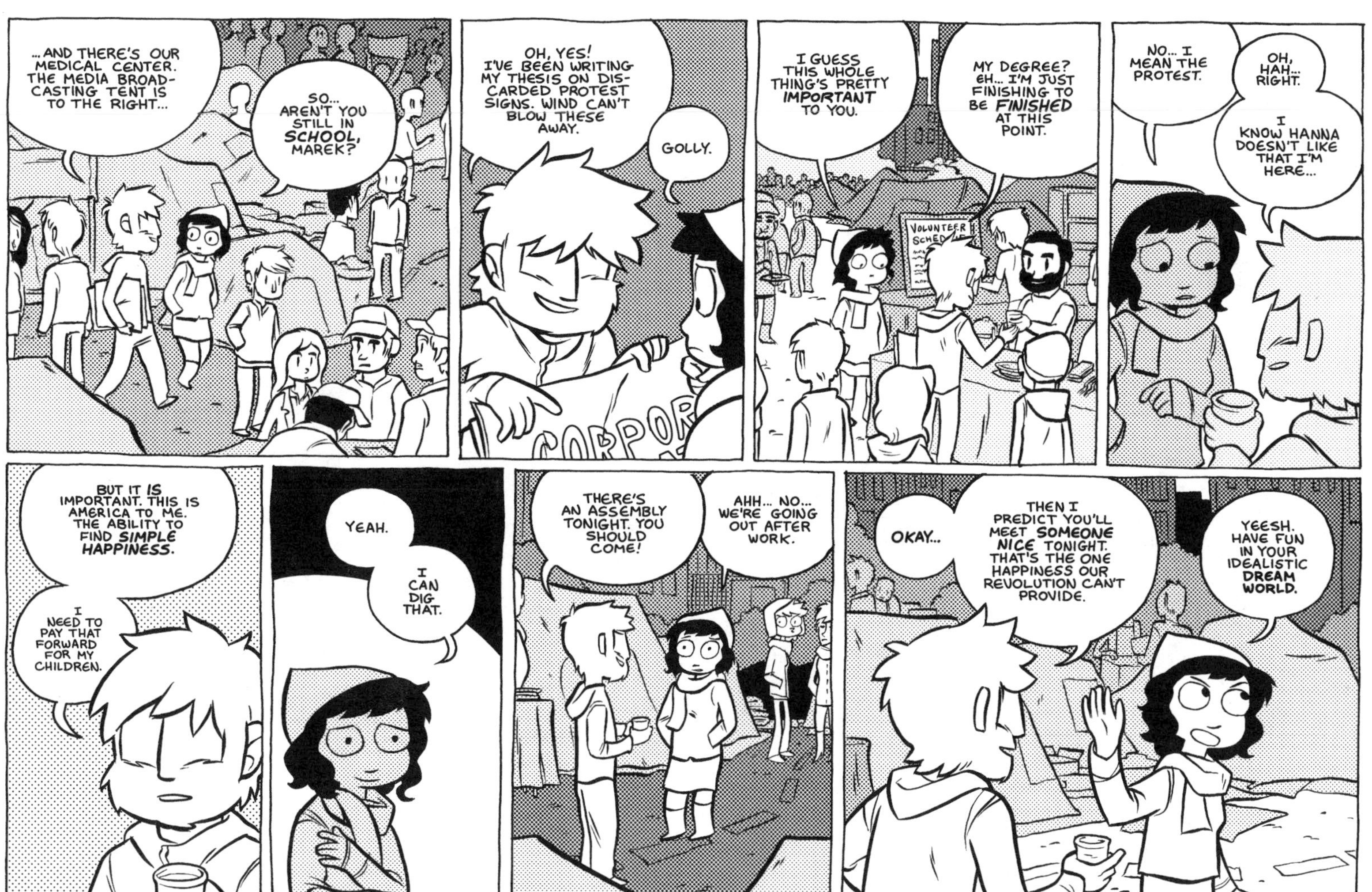
...AND THERE'S OUR MEDICAL CENTER. THE MEDIA BROADCASTING TENT IS TO THE RIGHT...
SO... AREN'T YOU STILL IN **SCHOOL,** MAREK?
OH, YES! I'VE BEEN WRITING MY THESIS ON DISCARDED PROTEST SIGNS. WIND CAN'T BLOW THESE AWAY.
GOLLY.
CORPOR
I GUESS THIS WHOLE THING'S PRETTY **IMPORTANT** TO YOU.
MY DEGREE? EH... I'M JUST FINISHING TO BE **FINISHED** AT THIS POINT.
VOLUNTEER SCHED
NO... I MEAN THE PROTEST.
OH, HAH... RIGHT.
I KNOW HANNA DOESN'T LIKE THAT I'M HERE...
BUT IT **IS** IMPORTANT. THIS IS AMERICA TO ME. THE ABILITY TO FIND **SIMPLE HAPPINESS.**
I NEED TO PAY THAT FORWARD FOR MY CHILDREN.
YEAH.
I CAN DIG THAT.
THERE'S AN ASSEMBLY TONIGHT. YOU SHOULD COME!
AHH... NO... WE'RE GOING OUT AFTER WORK.
OKAY...
THEN I PREDICT YOU'LL MEET **SOMEONE NICE** TONIGHT. THAT'S THE ONE HAPPINESS OUR REVOLUTION CAN'T PROVIDE.
YEESH. HAVE FUN IN YOUR IDEALISTIC **DREAM WORLD.**

THAT'S FOR YOU.
AHH! YOU'RE HERE TOO EARLY.
YOU CLOSE TOO LATE.
WE'RE SO UNDERSTAFFED THESE DAYS. USUALLY IT'S JUST ME AND OLLY.
IF ONLY I COULD GO BACK TO BEING HALF AS BUSY... AND COMPLAINING TWICE AS MUCH.
OOF. YEAH.
SO, BED & BODY WANTS ME ON FULL TIME... FOR A CORPORATE POSITION.
WHOA! ARE YOU..?
I ALREADY SAID YES.
WOW!
FOR SO LONG YOU WERE TALKING ABOUT QUITTING.
YEAH... WHAT A JOKE, HUH?
WHAT'S A JOKE?
...HOW I USED TO THINK LIKING WHAT I DO WOULD BE THE IMPORTANT PART.
AW, MAR...
THERE'S NO WAY WE'RE AT THAT PART OF THE NIGHT YET.

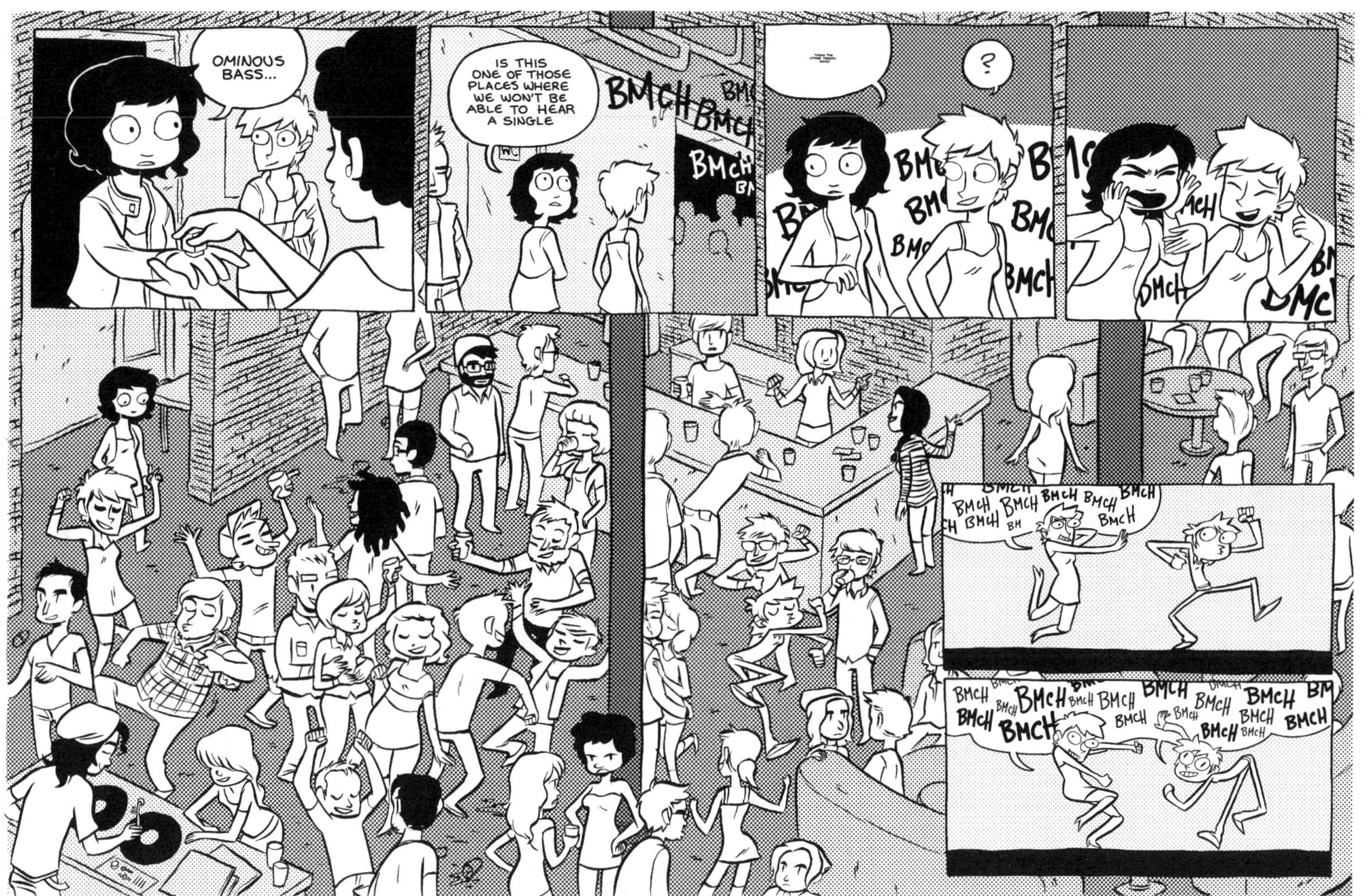

OMINOUS BASS...
IS THIS ONE OF THOSE PLACES WHERE WE WON'T BE ABLE TO HEAR A SINGLE
BMCH BMCH BMCH
BMCH
?
BMCH BMCH BMCH BMCH
BMCH BMCH

M... Mar...
I can't make it...
HAHA GEEZ, EVE!

HI GUYS.
WHOA HEY!
MARI-GOLD!
HEY.

DONOVAN! WHAT'VE YOU BEEN UP TO LATELY?
KEEPING BUSY. I'VE BEEN DOWN AT THE PROTESTS A LOT.

Oh!
Oh!
we were just there!!
HELPING OUT?

N-no, we...
WE WERE JUST PEERIN' AT THE FREAK SHOW.
HERE WE GO AGAIN.

SOME OF US WOULD RATHER COMPLAIN THAN MAKE AN ACTUAL DIFFERENCE.
SOME OF US THINK 'RE MAKING A FERENCE BY MPLAINING.
GuuUys...

Guys.
guys...

WHAT?!
...

How's it going.
OH CHRIST. IS SHE INTOXICATED BY THE RHYTHM?
MAYBE IF I ASK, THE DJ CAN PLAY IT BACKWARDS?

OH MAN. I LOVE THIS SONG.
DO YOU KNOW IT?
NOPE. BUT I LIKE IT!
GLAD THINGS ARE GOING WELL FOR YOU, MAR.

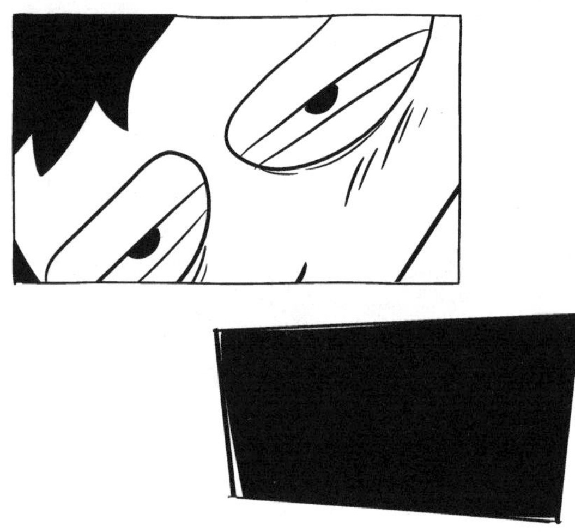

SO... HAVE YOU TALKED TO PARK LATELY?

AWW. WHY NOT? YOU SHOULD CALL HIM.

I GUESS YOU'VE HAD OTHER STUFF ON YOUR MIND...
GRAB
WAK!

...AND MAYBE YOU DIDN'T SAY GOODBYE ON THE BEST OF TERMS...

I JUST THINK HE'D LOVE TO HEAR FROM YOU.
DON'T DESTROY the AMERICAN DREAM

CAN YOU SERIOUSLY FAULT PEOPLE FOR WANTING A BETTER LIFE, HANNA?
I CAN FAULT THEIR DOPEY METHODS.

THERE MUST BE SOMETHING BETWEEN ANARCHY AND STATUS QUO THAT'S NOT COMPLETELY REPULS--
OH FUCK ME.
WOOOOOOOW!

GOOD GOD!
A WHOLE CLUB AND SHE SETTLES FOR PUGET SEAN?
NOT EVERYONE WANTS WHAT YOU WANT.

AND THIS IS WHY THE MOVEMENT ELUDES YOU. YOU THINK EVERYONE HAS THE SAME CHOICES AS YOU.
But it's beautiful, Hanna...

Love is beautiful

PEOPLE FUCK UP THEIR LIVES, DONOVAN. IT'S THEIR OWN FAULT.
PEOPLE'S LIVES CHANGE UNEXPECTEDLY! NO MATTER HOW IN CONTROL THEY FEEL.

YOU DON'T THINK IT COULD HAPPEN TO YOU?

I'M GETTIN' SICK IN HERE.

HONESTLY THOUGH, THEY LOOK DISGUSTING.
Sure do.

CAN I JUST SAY, DONOVAN... I THINK IT'S GREAT WHAT YOU'RE DOING.
THANK YOU.

YOU'D THINK EXPLAINING IT TO FRIENDS WOULD BE EASIER.
DUDE... IT MAKES SO MUCH **SENSE!**

IT'S LIKE...
THINGS KEEP GETTING WORSE... AND I NEVER EVEN **THINK** ABOUT IT 'TIL IT HAPPENS.

THAT'S WHAT THE UNCHECKED POWERS DO.
TAKE YOUR RIGHTS AWAY SO **GRADUALLY** YOU DON'T EVEN **NOTICE.**
THEY HAVE NO REASON TO STOP.
I KNOW...
BUT I NEVER PAY ATTENTION!

IT'S NOT TOO LATE.
THIS IS A GREAT TIME TO ARTICULATE OUR NEEDS. TO TRULY PURSUE HAPPINESS.

IT SEEMS SO OBVIOUS WHEN YOU **TALK** ABOUT IT, RIGHT?

GOD, YOU'RE SO HOT

YOU'RE A **HOT MESS.**

HEY MAN. HAVE YOU SEEN MARI-GOLD?
YES.
I SAW HER LEAVE.
WHA?
THE THREE OF THEM LEFT TOGETHER.
OH.
GUESS SHE WAS TIRED.
...AND IT'S A HIGHER SALARY, SO I CAN PROBABLY MOVE, AND...
FUCK! MAYBE I'LL GET MY OWN PLACE!
OH! AND YOU GUYS
HEALTH INSURANCE! CAN YOU IMAGINE?
YES.
NOPE!
...AND VACATION DAYS?!
SO FUCKIN' RAD!

AND ALL YOU GOTTA DO IS SETTLE FOR THE LIFE YOU NEVER WANTED.
HANNA!

NO...
THAT MIGHT BE TRUE.

BUT I KNOW IT'S GOING TO BE FINE, GUYS.
'CAUSE LIKE... I CAN FEEL MYSELF CHANGING.

I CAN ACCEPT WHAT I DON'T LIKE. THE THINGS I **DO** LIKE DON'T **EMBARRASS** ME ANYMORE.
I'M NOT CHASING HAPPINESS NOW... IT'S **CATCHING UP** TO ME.

I'M BECOMING MY MOTHER AND I'M COMPLETELY ALL RIGHT WITH IT.
I'LL JUST KEEP ADDING COMFORT TO MY LIFE 'TIL I'VE GOT COMFORT TO SPARE.

AND THEN I'M GONNA BE A MOM, YOU GUYS.
WHEN THINGS GET EASY ENOUGH.

I'M GONNA BE SUCH A FUCKING MOM

Z

AH HA HA... I CAN'T BREATHE
HA HA
HA HA HA
I LOVE YOU.
PLEASE NEVER LEAVE ME TO BECOME A GROWN-UP.
OH, I WON'T.
I JUST WANT TO BE LOVED.
THAT'S THE ONLY PART OF THE DREAM I'VE FIGURED OUT.
WHAT'D I JUST SAY? YOU'RE WELCOME, BITCH.
NO! HA HA! NO I JUST MEAN...
I WANNA BE A PERSON WHO DESERVES TO BE LOVED.
WELL, GOOD LUCK THEN.

Y'KNOW, EVE... I'M NEVER GONNA HAVE KIDS.
AWW..!
YOU SURE?
BUT YOU'D BE SUCH A FUN MOM!
I'VE BEEN HIGH FOR 61,320 HOURS.
... 61,321.
EH HEH...
EVERYTHING IN MY LIFE WOULD BE OBSTRUCTED BY PARENTHOOD. I'VE ALREADY FOUND HAPPINESS.
WELL, THAT'S A GOOD THING, RIGHT?

...HAVE YOU AND MAREK AGREED ON IT?
WE'LL HAVE TO, EVENTUALLY.

BUT I SHOULD'VE BEEN HERE.
WHY?

YOU WOULD'VE HATED IT.
WHY WOULD I WANNA DO THAT TO YOU?

I SHOULD'VE BEEN HERE.
I'M ALL RIGHT, HANNA. IT'S NOTHING WE CAN'T REPLACE.
POLICE

ARE PEOPLE STICKING AROUND?
YEAH. WE'RE GONNA FIGURE OUT WHERE TO GO NEXT.

CAN I STAY A LITTLE WHILE?
I DON'T WANNA BE IN THE WAY.
OF COURSE.

STAY AS LONG AS YOU WANT.

37

HEY! JACOB!

CAN YOU PLEASE SCRATCH MY BACK?
IT'S DRIVING ME BANANAS!

OHH YES
SCRATCH SCRATCH

SO THIS IS WHAT MAKING LOVE TO YOU IS LIKE.
SCRATCH SCRATCH
SCRATCH

EWW!
CHRIST, JACOB!

"MAKING LOVE."

SAY, HAVE YOU NOTICED THIS SONG PLAYING EVERYWHERE RECENTLY?
AW YEAH. RIGHT THERE
SAL
OFF!

GOOD TRACK N' ALL... ALWAYS SEEMED KINDA AMBIENT FOR THE AIRWAVES.
IT'S SUPER-MARKET MUSIC.
SAL
OFF!

I CAN WITHHOLD MY OPINION OR GIVE YOU SCRATCHES.
WHILE NOTICEABLY MORE AMBIENT T ITS ACCOMPANY TRACKS, THE SON POP QUALITIES A INDISPUTABLE

SCRATCH
SCRATCH
SCRATCH
EMPLOYEES ONLY
NO!

C'MON... DREMEL...

I WAS SURE WE HAD A PINEAPPLE IN HE--

AGENT 437!!

M... MIKE VAN MONT-PELIER?!
IS THE ROOM SECURE?!

WHA..? I DON'T KNOW! HOW'RE YOU GETTING SIGNAL IN HERE?!
THERE'S NO TIME FOR THAT! LISTEN.
I NEED YOU TO MAKE SURE THERE'S NO ONE IN THE ROOM WITH YOU.
RIGHT!

SLAM

SCRATCH
SCRATCH
SCRATCH
SCRATCH
SCRATCH
SCRATCH

THIS SONG'S ALL OVER THE PLACE LATELY. FEELS PRETTY NOSTALGIC, HUH?

THOUGH PERSONALLY I PREFER THEIR EARLIER WORK.
JANE!

GOOD TO SEE-- HEY, CAN YOU SCRATCH MY BACK WHILE YOU'RE THERE?

SO, EVE. YOU HUNG UP ON MIKE.
HE WAS ALMOST PRACTICALLY ANNOYED BY THAT.
LOOK, WHATEVER IT IS... I DON'T HAVE TIME FOR IT.

SCRATCH MY BACK?
CAN I JUST TELL YOU WHAT IT IS? AS A FAVOR?

OH FINE. WHAT IS I--
PRESS

AAAAAAA
SPLAT
MAN, I'M SORRY. I JUST GOT THIS THING TODAY.
...OF COURSE...
WHOA! IS THIS THE 2ND AVENUE TUNNEL?
YUP. WE USE THIS SPACE FOR A LOT OF THINGS.
WON'T THAT BE A PROBLEM WHEN THEY PUT THE TRAINS IN?
A LOT OF THINGS WILL BE PROBLEMS IN 200 YEARS.
TELL ME, EVE... HAVE YOU HEARD OF THAT NEW COFFEE PLACE, THE OIL CAN?
OH YEAH, THE ONE NEAR YOUR WORK.
IS IT ANY GOOD?
IT IS DECIDEDLY NOT GOOD.

LEMME GUESS... THE GUILD OF THE RISTRETTO'S AFRAID OF A LITTLE COMPETITION.
COM-PETITION WE CAN HANDLE.

THE FOUNDER OF THE OIL CAN IS MARCUS TOTH.
HE WAS PART OF AN ELITE STAFF WE WERE TRAINING, FOR A NEW GUILD INITIATIVE.

BUT TWO WEEKS AFTER HIS TRAINING, HE ABRUPTLY QUIT AND OPENED HIS ROASTERY.
PRETTY CONVENIENT, HUH? HE EVEN SNIPED THREE OF OUR EMPLOYEES.
LOCAL CAFE TRAINS EMPLOYEES
NEW BARISTAS "EXCITED"
CAFE TRAINING 'GOING WELL'
EMPLOYEE QUITS
"I QUIT"
WHOTTA DICK!

WORST OF ALL, THOUGH, HE STOLE AN ESATTAMENTE SCALE FROM GUILD HEAD-QUARTERS. A RARE ARTIFACT WITH THE POWER TO MEASURE TASTE ITSELF.
POLICE BLOTTER
OIL CAN

BUT WHAT DOES THIS HAVE TO DO WITH--
K-! K!
SCRATCH
SCRATCH
SCRATCH

THE DISTRESS OF THE GUILD IS BECOMING PALPABLE, AND...
THAT'S WHAT ITCHES? MY TATTOO?

IT'S... Y'KNOW. LIKE HARRY POTTER.
GUH

...SO IF I HELP YOU WITH ALL THIS, THE ITCHING WILL GO AWAY.
YUP.

THIS IS... SO VERY STUPID
YAY!!
SCRATCH SCRATCH

EVERY-ONE, THIS IS EVE.

SHE'LL BE OUR SNEAKING SPECIALIST. SHE'S SMALL AND FITS INTO PLACES.
I DO?

MORRIS IS OUR NERD SPECIALIST. HE TYPES ON THE COMPUTER AND EXPLAINS A LOT OF THINGS.
GREETINGS, FEMALE. HAVE YOU SEEN STAR WARS?

DON IS OUR FIGHT SPECIALIST. HE'S A CERTIFIED REALLY REALLY REALLY GOOD FIGHTER.
YOU DON'T NEED TO BE SO TECHNICAL ABOUT IT.

AND I'M THE COOL ONE. ANY QUESTIONS BEFORE WE BEGIN?
WHAT ARE WE DOING?

OH RIGHT. THE PLAN IS TO BREAK INTO THE OIL CAN'S CORPORATE OFFICE AT NIGHTFALL. BUT FIRST, WE NEED SOME PASSCODE INFORMATION FROM THE SHOP ITSELF.

THAT'S WHERE YOU COME IN, EVE.
NONE OF THEIR BARISTAS WILL RECOG-NIZE YOU.

AS LONG AS WE'RE DISCREET THIS SHOULD BE PRETTY CUT-AND-DRIED.

YOU LOOK COOL AS HELL IN THOSE, JANE.
THANKS!
...BUT I'M NOT GETTING A READING FROM OUR WIRETAP. IT'S LIKE SOMEONE'S BLOCKING THE SIGNAL.
MAYBE THEY'RE USING A NOISE GATE TO BLOCK OUT SOUND... MUCH LIKE BILBO USES BLANKETS TO SHROUD HIMSELF FROM SAURON'S EYE.
HA HA WHAT? DID YOU SAY "BILBO"?
YOU SILLY GOOSE! BILBO NEVER TOUCHES A PALANTIR.
WHAT KIND OF NERD ARE YOU?
BKAM!
HA HAHA HA HA HA HA HA HA HA HAHA
HA HA HA! HA! HA HA

PULL

GOD DAMN IT!
I KNEW HE WAS A WEAK, LAZY CARICATURE OF NERD CULTURE!

WH- WHAT NOW..?
THERE'S A LOOSE GRATE AROUND HERE SOMEWHERE...
HEY GUYS! UP HERE!

I THINK I CAN GET THIS OPEN IF WE--

BKAM!

BKAM!

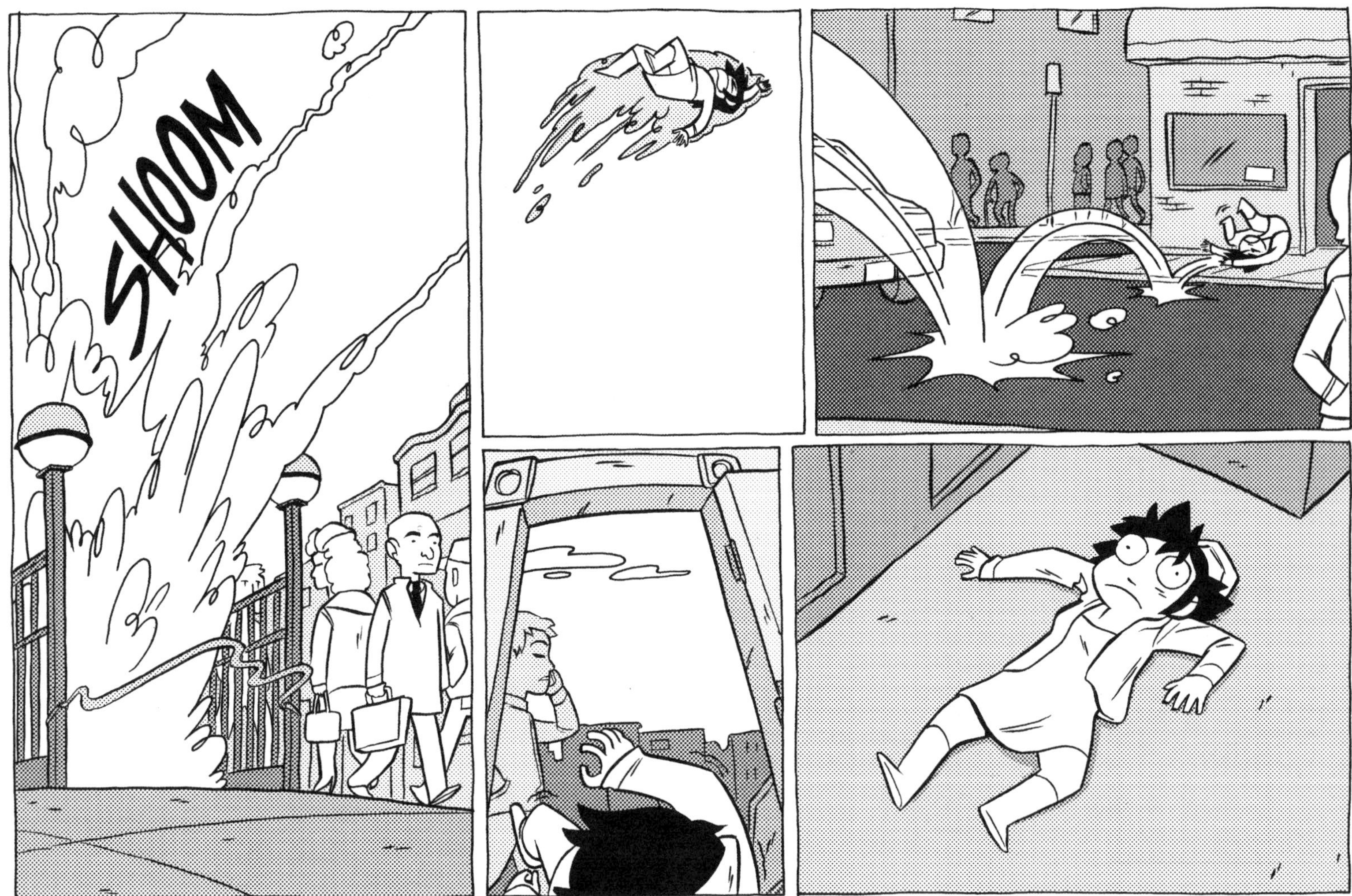
SHOOM

THE
EST. 2012
OIL CAN

WHAT CAN I GET YOU?

A SHOT TO GO..?

TIP

WE DON'T DO THOSE TO GO.
F-FOR HERE, THEN...

ONE SHOT COMING UP.
TAMP TAMP TAMP
HERE YOU GO.
UH...
LEMME KNOW HOW YOU LIKE IT.
CH-CRAK

THAT... SONG...
SHE'S WAKIN' UP, BOSS.
LOOKS LIKE YOU TOOK A NASTY FALL. CAN I GET YOU SOME ASPIRIN? A TINCTURE?
HOW 'BOUT A MARTINI WITH A FIST?
FIGHT
DON!
I'M FREED!
C'MON EVE! NO TIME TO THANK ME.
ALTERCATE

HOW DID YOU FIND ME, DON?
I JUST FOLLOWED THAT STUPID SONG. THERE'S TROUBLE WHEREVER IT PLAYS!

WELL, THAT WAS SOME IMPRESSIVE FIGHTING IN THERE!
AH, THANKS. JUST DOIN' WHAT'S--

OH, NO... THE EXPLOSION-- YOU'RE HURT!

IT'S JUST... MY STRONGNESS RECEPTORS HAVE BEEN WEAKENED. I CAN ONLY FIGHT HALF AS GOOD.
...IN LAYMAN'S TERMS?

I CAN DEFEAT MAYBE TWO GUYS, TOPS.
SHIT!

WE NEED TO FIND JANE! REGROUPING IS OUR ONLY HOPE.
THERE'S AN ABOVE-GROUND HIDEOUT TEN BLOCKS FROM HERE...
PERFECT!

...BUT IT'S TEN BLOCKS WEST.
OHH NOOOO OOO OO
THERE THEY ARE!

DO YOU HAVE ANOTHER HIDEOUT IN GUAM? SURE WE COULDN'T ZIP UP TO THERE?
I DON'T KNOW, EVE

OH, HERE. THIS CORNER.

THERE THEY GO!

AH... CAN I GET TWO BACK?

LET'S GO.

TRY NOT TO RUN TOO FAST OR WALK TOO SLOW. **SAUNTER.**

BE COOL.

THEY'RE BEHIND US.
RIGHT.

ON THE COUNT OF THREE... I WANT YOU TO HOLD THIS AND STAND COMPLETELY STILL.
HUH?
THREE!

HEY! WAIT!!
THAT WAS SO NOT EVEN COUNTING!

TWONG

HA HA!
POK
AAAAAAAAAAA

SPLOT
HA
HA HA
HA HA HA!
HA HA HA!
HA HA
NO.
CREAK
'BOUT TIME. GET IN HERE!
NICE TO SEE YOU ALIVE, TOO.
IT WASN'T SUPPOSED TO GO LIKE THIS! OUR COVER IS BLOWN. WE'LL NEVER GET THROUGH MARCUS' SECURITY SYSTEM NOW!
DARN!
EVE AND I MADE IT TO THE SHOP...
OH?
BUT THEY POISONED ME, AND WE HAD TO RUN FOR OUR LIVES!
EVE, DID YOU SEE THEM OPEN HIDDEN DOORS? TYPE IN ANY SECURITY CODES?
NO. I WAS UNCONSCIOUS!
THE LAST THING I SAW WAS SOME SHOWY BARISTA--
MIKE! IS THIS A USB ESPRESSO MACHINE?
WELL, SURE! ...BUT WHY?

PLEASE ENTER
LOGIN ID

TAMP
TAMP
TAMP

IDENTIFICATION COMPLETE.
WELCOME!
Oilcan:~ bigdong$
OOH
YES!

THIS IS IT! WE'LL HAVE ONE CHANCE TO GET INTO MARCUS' LAIR AND FIND THAT SCALE.

OH RIGHT. I FORGOT ABOUT THE SCALE.
WHO KNOWS WHAT HE'LL DO WITH THAT POWER.

BUT WE ONLY HAVE ACCESS TO THE UPPER FLOORS. WE NEED TO GET DOWN TO THAT OFFICE, SOMEHOW...
WELL, GLAD I COULD HELP! I'M OFF THE HOOK, RIGHT?

YES... OF COURSE! WE'LL USE A GRAPPLING HOOK!
HEY... DON'T ACT LIKE I'M VOLUNTEERING!

YOU'RE VOLUNTEERING? WHAT A CHAMP!
OMG

THE KEY TO MARCUS' OFFICE IS IN THE NORTH-FACING FILE DRAWER.
THIS WIRE IS FULLY RETRACTABLE. IF YOU RUN INTO ANY TROUBLE DOWN THERE, ONE SWIFT TUG WILL BRING YOU BACK UP.
RIGHT...
IT'S A NOBLE THING YOU'RE DOING, EVE. IT MEANS SO MUCH FOR THE GUILD.
YOU THINK SO?
'CAUSE I WON'T LIE... THIS FEELS LIKE THE MOST MEANINGLESS THING I'VE EVER DON--
HERE YOU GO!

SCRAMBLE
SCRAMBLE

JACK..!

YES?
SHIT!!

GET UP, EVE.
IT'S YOU
OF COURSE IT'S YOU

SO, YOU'RE HERE TO TAKE DOWN MARCUS. OLD MAN MIKE SENT YOU?

IF I'D'VE KNOWN YOU'D BE...

TOSS

I WASN'T IN A PLACE TO SAY NO TO MARCUS. HE OFFERED ME A BETTER WAGE AND FULL-TIME HOURS.
HE HASN'T COME THROUGH ON **EITHER**.

BESIDES, HIS--
WELL... WHATEVER. SCREW HIM.

POINT IS I MISS MY JOB, AND JANEY AND ALL THOSE GUYS.
I MISS MY FRIENDS.

I'D APPRECIATE IT.
I'LL TELL THEM YOU SAID SO.

YOU REALLY **ARE** A GOOD GUY, JACK. IN SPITE OF HOW BAD YOU SUCK.
I GUESS I'LL TAKE THAT.

TO BE HONEST, I WAS HOPING THEY'D SEND YOU.
OH YEAH?
YEAH. THERE'S SO MUCH WE LEFT UNRESOLVED.
YOU KNOW, THERE'S NO ONE ELSE HERE.
WE SHOULD TOTALLY MAKE LOVE.
TUG

KRASH

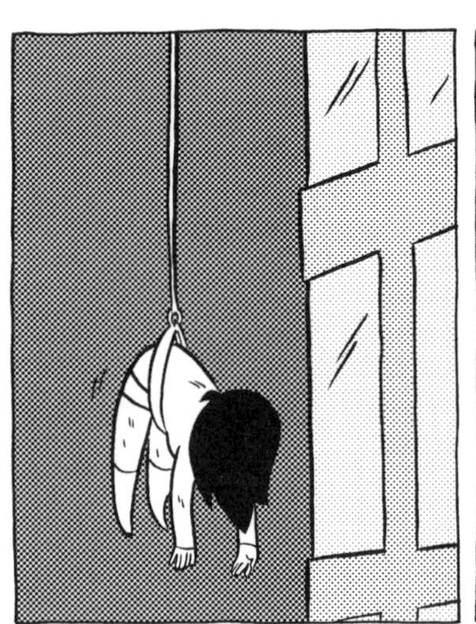

TECH 20 TOP COOL BUSINESSES
PLUG'D IN!
yelp
NIFTY AWARD

PRIVATE

WELCOME TO MY **WHEELHOUSE,** AGENT 437.
Roas
Grind&
Drink.

THE NAME'S MARCUS. WON'T YOU HAVE A **DRINK?**

THANK YOU

I KNEW THE GUILD WOULD TRY TO RECLAIM MY SCALE, AS A TOKEN FOR THEIR BITTERNESS.

BUT IT'S RIGHTFULLY MINE. THE GUILD PROFITED FROM MY TALENT.
YOU WERE THERE FOR TWO WEEKS.
THEY SHOULD BE GRATEFUL. IT WAS INEVITABLE I'D STAKE OUT ON MY OWN!

I JUST HAD THE STEREO INSTALLED. ISN'T THIS SONG TOTALLY BANGIN'?

I'VE HEARD IT EVERYWHERE LATELY!
OH REALLY, YOU'VE HEARD IT?

PROBABLY 'CAUSE I PLAY IT AT THE SHOP SO MUCH. IT'S BASICALLY MY ANTHEM.
WAIT...

YOU KNOW THIS SONG CAME OUT, LIKE... SEVEN YEARS AGO, RIGHT?

O...OF COURSE I KNOW THAT! IT-- IT'S AUGHTIES VINTAGE!
RIGHT

I'M BRINGING IT BACK!
HA HA OKAY

LOOK, I'LL FORGIVE YOUR HIPSTER OUTBURSTS. I'M A REGULAR, UNPRETENTIOUS DUDE.

BUT WHY AREN'T YOU DRINKING THAT COFFEE, AS IT RAPIDLY COOLS?!
OH, RIGHT, I...

SIIIP

GUH

PTTHHH! PTOO! YOU POISONED ME AGAIN!

"POISON"? WHAT AM I, PSYCHOTIC?
THAT'S A FRESH POT.

...AND WHAT DO YOU MEAN "AGAIN"?

PEER

...ARE YOU SURE IT ISN'T POISON?
KILL HER

WAIT... WAIT!

MY MISSION HAS CHANGED. I NO LONGER NEED YOUR SCALE.

I JUST NEED YOU TO ADMIT YOU'RE AN ASSHOLE.

HOW ON EARTH AM I AN ASSHOLE?!

YOU RIPPED OFF THE GUILD FOR YOUR OWN PROFIT.
WITH THE TRAINING? SO WHAT?
YOU CAN'T COPYRIGHT AN IDEA.

NO, BUT YOU CAN BE AN ASSHOLE ABOUT IT.
•REC

SO YOU'RE SAYING I'M AN ASSHOLE
YES.

YOU'LL REALLY LEAVE ME ALONE IF I SAY IT?

NOD

HEH..
WELL...
SELF DESTRUCT CLASSIC™
NEVER!!
BLAM

SO, WAIT. ARE YOU SAYING THOSE PEOPLE *DIED?*

I DON'T KNOW... THEY *EXPLODED.*
YOU DON'T KNOW.

ANYWAY, THE GUILD SEEMS HAPPY. I GET FREE LATTE ART FOR *LIFE,* OR SOME-THING.

BUT I BLEW AN *ENTIRE WEEKEND* ON THAT MISSION. I HAVE TO WORK IN *TWO HOURS!*

PLUS, GET THIS -- WE BEAT MARCUS, YET MY BACK IS *STILL ITCHING.*
WORSE THAN *BEFORE!*

MAYBE MY BODY'S TELLING ME I'VE STRETCHED TOO *THIN.* THAT I CAN'T OFFER SO *MUCH* OF MYSELF TO OTHER PEOPLE.

NOPE, YOU HAVE A SUPER GROSS RASH.
WHAT!!

38

OH MAN. SO EXCITED.
THE TRICK IS GETTING THERE BEFORE THE COMMUTER RUSH.

MUST BE AN AMAZING PLACE.
OH, IT IS. WE EAT HERE LIKE EVERY DAY!

SO THAT'S WHAT YOU CALL THIS HOUR... "DAY."

THE USUAL FOR BOTH OF US, JON.
HOW 'BOUT YOU, AIMEE?
NO

JUST COFFEE. I'LL EAT ON MY WAY HOME.
YOU SURE?

OH MY GOD. SO GOOD.
IT'S EXTRA GOOD TODAY!

WHAT'S IN IT?

EGGS.
I WANNA SAY SALT.

I TELL YOU WHAT, AIMEE -- AND I'VE LIVED ALL OVER. NO CITY BUT NEW YORK UNDERSTANDS A SIMPLE BREAKFAST.
UH HUH

THE LONGER YOU LIVE HERE, THE MORE YOU'LL APPRECIATE THAT.
DUDE!

I'M FROM ITHACA. NOT MARS!
UH... LET'S GET YOUR THINGS, AIMEE...

GOD!

WHY DID I LET THAT STRESS ME OUT SO MUCH?!
LARRY'S A LITTLE INTENSE, IT'S--

MY EX DID THAT SHIT, TOO! TRYING TO EDUCATE ME ON STUFF HE'D JUST FIGURED OUT. LIKE IT MADE HIM SO MUCH SMARTER THAN ME!

OH, YOU FOUND A WAY TO MANAGE YOUR LIFE? COOL. CONGRATS.
STOP FUCKING TELLING ME ABOUT IT!

YOU'RE LECTURING THE AIR.
I KNOW.

C'MON... HERE.
NO, I--
DON'T LEAVE THIS WAY.

I GUESS I NEED SOME NEW EXPERIENCES OF MY OWN. SOMETHING THAT SHIFTS **MY** BEHAVIOR.

NOTHING WRONG WITH THAT.

BUT ISN'T IT JUST A ***DANGLING CARROT?***
NOBODY BACK **HOME** SEES ANYTHING NEW IN ME. THEY JUST THINK I'M ***JADED.***

WHY'S IT IMPORTANT FOR ***THEM*** TO SEE A CHANGE?
I DUNNO...
SO I DON'T FEEL LIKE I'M ***CRAZY?***

THEN YOU'LL BE CHASING THAT CARROT FOR A ***LONG*** TIME.
IT'S NOT EVEN A ***GOOD*** CARROT.

FOR WHAT IT'S WORTH... I'VE SEEN THE BIGGEST CHANGES WHEN THINGS ARE THE LEAST COMFORTABLE.
IT'S NEVER A WELCOME FEELING.

WITH MY MOST RECENT GIRLFRIEND... IT ALMOST FELT LIKE A GOOD PLACE.
THE EASE OF IT KINDA TOOK ME BY SURPRISE.

BUT SHE STARTED TO EXPECT MORE, AND I PULLED AWAY.
AND SHE CLEARLY SENSED THAT, AND PUSHED HARDER.

I CAN'T EVEN DESCRIBE WHY I HAD TO LEAVE SO BADLY. I WANTED TO DATE MORE PEOPLE, I GUESS.

AND HAVE YOU?

WE'RE "NOT TALKING ABOUT THAT"... RIGHT?
RIGHT...

I'D LIKE THINGS TO BE SIMPLE. BUT THEY WON'T BE, UNTIL I FIGURE SOME THINGS OUT... OR JUST STOP CARING.

IF I KNEW HOW TO INVEST IN THE FUTURE WITHOUT MISSING OUT ON THE PRESENT, I WOULD.

BUT HERE I AM IN AN UNMADE BED, MARINATING IN MY **WET CLOTHES**.
TAKE THEM OFF.

WHAT'S YOUR **SATURDAY** LOOKIN' LIKE?
DUNNO. THERE WAS SOME BREAD BAKING CLASS I WANTED TO DO IN THE CITY LATER, BUT...
I DON'T **KNOW**...
I'M ALL TIRED AND **DISTRACTED** N' SHIT.
GO TO THE CLASS, YA FORLORN LIL' **BITCH!**
SMACK

YOU'RE
A BITCH!

DICK.

SLAM!

LARRY HAS SO MUCH PORN TO WATCH.

Meredith Gran makes comics and teaches at the School of Visual Arts. She lives in Brooklyn and is thinking of painting her bike soon.

Read more *Octopus Pie* online at:
www.octopuspie.com